# Under the Enchanter

Nina Beachcroft, whose ancestors were related to Jane Austen, read English at Oxford, and published her first children's novel in 1972. She is married to a doctor, and they have two daughters. The family live on a village green in Hertfordshire.

Also by
Nina Beachcroft in Piccolo

Nina Beachcroft

# Under the Enchanter

**Piccolo** Pan Books
in association with Heinemann

First published 1974 by William Heinemann Ltd
This edition published 1979 by Pan Books Ltd,
Cavaye Place, London SW10 9PG
in association with William Heinemann Ltd
© Nina Beachcroft 1974
ISBN 0 330 25648 3
Made and printed in Great Britain by
Cox & Wyman Ltd, London, Reading and Fakenham

# one

'I wonder if being born feels a bit like this,' thought Laura gloomily as she clambered stiffly out from the back seat of the car. After five hours it had become so warm, so home-like, so comfortably bestrewn with comics, sweet papers and biscuit crumbs. If one was born and left the safe protection of the womb, there would be the same shock of cold fresh air, the same staggery feeling in the legs. But of course, she thought, as her feet touched the ground, the staggery leg part was wrong, she must be likening the birth to that of a baby foal or calf, rather than a human baby: they simply lay and shrieked.

'Hideous, naked, piping loud . . .' She preferred foals.

'Come on, Laura, don't dream,' said her mother briskly. 'You can carry something down.'

'Can't we get the car in through the gate?' asked Laura. 'The house is miles away, right over the field. We'll *die*, carrying all that heavy stuff down. Look, there's a sort of track going across.'

Her father had parked the car just by the gate that said 'Ramshead Lodge' on it.

'You're right,' he said. 'I think I can do it, and it will get the car off the road, but it will be a tight fit.'

'You can watch the gatepost on your side, Laura,' said her mother. Then too late, 'Laura! Andrew!'

But Laura and her younger brother Andrew were already halfway across the field.

The house faced them as they ran up to it. It was an old grey stone farmhouse, battered, yet pleasing to the eye. A few flagstones made a path along the side of the house to the stables, which were part of the house at one end; a few big daisies stood in clumps about the front door, otherwise it was simply a house in a field, without garden or garage.

'It's good,' announced Andrew, drawing breath outside

the front door. 'I think we're going to have an all right sort of holiday here.'

'It's super!' agreed Laura enthusiastically, her spirits already rising considerably. They had not been really low; it was simply that she always felt like this when she was tired and hungry and just reborn from a car. 'And stables, Andrew, do you see? Do you think there are any horses?'

'Of course not,' said Andrew scornfully. 'Who would look after them? This place must be empty a lot, especially in the winter.'

The car slowly bumped down over the rough grass to stand beside them. Laura's and Andrew's parents got out, exclaiming at the greenness and the freshness and the quietness and the beautiful smells – all the remarks which people who have been in London for the past year do make.

'Look at the date of the house, 1667, carved above the front door,' said Mrs Hearst, coming to stand beside her children.

'There's an inscription in Latin too,' said Andrew. 'Look, it's rather faint and chipped away, but you can see it all right.'

The Latin words said:

Num mea
Mox huius
Sed postea
Nescio quius

' "Now mine",' translated Andrew, then stuck; although his school was of the kind which had been teaching him Latin from an early age.

'Well, don't look at me,' said Laura, whose very modern comprehensive school did not include Latin among all its other subjects.

'It's simple,' said their father coming up behind them.

'Now mine
 Soon his

6

But afterwards
I don't know whose'

'Oh, I remember. Mrs Anderson mentioned this over the telephone,' said Mrs Hearst. 'The house was built by a woman for her son to live in after her. I've even been told her name except that I can't remember it now. Let's get inside. The key should be in a little box down by the door-scraper, it is always kept there for the next visitor, Mrs Anderson said.'

There indeed, on a nest of moss, was the box. But there was no key inside.

They stood forlornly, suitcases piled about them.

'How extremely annoying of Mrs Anderson,' said Mrs Hearst at last. 'We'll have to go to the farm. I think it must be over that field, partly hidden by the trees there.'

'What about the back?' suggested Laura. She was just setting off to investigate when Andrew calmly opened the front door.

'It was in the lock all the time,' he announced triumphantly. 'Don't know what you lot would do without me, really.'

Inside the house it was cold and dark and fusty after the bright evening sunshine.

'What a depressing number of little rag mats,' said Mrs Hearst after a moment's inspection. 'But it looks reasonably clean, anyway. I'd better have a look at the kitchen and turn on the electricity so we can have some hot water. There's no fridge, but what a lovely large pantry ...' Her voice died away in the distance as she investigated it.

Meanwhile Laura and Andrew raced through all the rooms, first downstairs, then up. The furniture was sparse and interesting, mostly dating from the nineteen-thirties and obviously bought in cheaply at local sales. There was a big table and a sideboard and an assortment of chairs in the living room into which the front door had opened and out of which was the staircase to the upper part of the house. At the far side of the living room Andrew found a door leading to a dusty little parlour with a broken sofa, a stopped clock on the mantelpiece and a bookcase with books and a pile of old magazines in it.

Then they thundered up the uncarpeted stairs and found four bedrooms, one of which had been turned into a bathroom. There were long interesting looking drip stains under the bath taps and a large dead spider lying in the exact centre of the bath. Someone had left behind the grubby remains of a bar of soap in the wash-basin.

'Bags I this bedroom,' cried Laura, excited at finding one tucked away by itself up a little flight of steps at one end of the house. It gave her a special feeling of privacy and apartness to have such a room. She stuck her head out of the window and found herself not so very high up, all the bedroom windows were within easy jumping distance of the ground. You never knew, this might be useful in a fire. Or if a murderer crept stealthily into one's room in the middle of the night.

To the right hand of Laura came the stables and at the end of the stables a stone wall with a stile through to the next field. To the left was Andrew's room, then the large room with a double bed in it, which was obviously suitable for their parents.

'There's no back to this house,' announced Andrew when they met downstairs again.

'Don't be silly, whatever do you mean?'

'Why, that none of the windows look out at the back and there is no back door.'

'There must be,' said Laura, going to investigate. But he was right. There wasn't. The house had its back to the hills and looked only south-west into the valley. Its rear wall was blank and depressing with only one very small window to it, the pantry window, beneath which were several feet of high nettles.

Then back in the living room Andrew found a note addressed to his parents. It was from Mrs Anderson, the owner of the house, containing necessary instructions as to the whereabouts of things such as electricity meters and, at the end, a sentence: 'Please feed William if you see him!!!'

'Who is William?' Andrew asked.

'Gracious, I don't know. We'd better ask Mummy.'

Mrs Hearst when shown the note was equally baffled.

'How extraordinary, Mrs Anderson never mentioned a William. Is he a person or an animal? And where is he, anyway? I wonder why he needs three exclamation marks?'

'I don't think he can be in the house,' said Andrew thoughtfully. 'I've looked into every cupboard now.'

It should be by this time obvious that Ramshead Lodge had long ago ceased being a workaday farm and was used only for holidays; the holidays of Mrs Anderson, the owner, her family, her friends, and the friends of her friends. The friends of friends were charged a small sum per week. The Hearsts were friends of friends and had never actually met Mrs Anderson. They lived in a southern suburb of London and this was their first trip north, at least as far as Laura and Andrew were concerned. Somehow, previously all their connections had taken them south and west of London and once they had been over the Channel to France. And so the keen air and high moors and hills of the north had remained a closed book to them. But now the pages were opening . . . Laura, for one, resolved to enjoy the holiday to its full; to bask in the full atmosphere of northernness. She would paddle in ice-cold streams and tarns, she would roll in the heather and listen to the lonely cries of the – peewits? no, curlews? oh – whatever lonely birds there were, crying about the place. She would commune with Nature: whatever that was.

'To the North, to the North!' She had read out each sign-post in a hypnotic chant as they drove past it up the A1 until her family with one voice told her to shut up.

The A1, as Laura herself had to admit, had been mostly rather dull: the country they passed on their northern voyage uninspiring. But at last they had turned off the main road and entered a land of stone walls and houses and quiet market towns and villages; the country rolled and heaved and then in the distance came their first sight of the hills. The road wound up and down beside a river and the hills came nearer until their car was right underneath their bare windswept tops. Even the weather changed; it had been overcast and warm, now it was fresher, and the clouds had broken up, and they and their shadows beneath them were moving briskly down the broad valley. The light turned much bluer and golder, the racing clouds whiter.

'Of course we really ought to have come by train,' Laura had said, hanging half out of the car window. 'All proper holidays, in books I mean, begin with train journeys and arriving at little wayside stations and being met. And one's parents shouldn't be there at all; the children should be sent off on their own for some reason, to stay with wild cousins, or a mad old aunt. Why can't we have holidays like that?'

Her parents laughed. 'Sorry we can't oblige you by disappearing, but we have our uses, you know,' her mother had said, while her father pointed out that in any case it would be impossible to arrive up here by rail as the railway had been discontinued years ago.

'Perhaps it's now a ghost line and there's a ghost train that whistles by on it in the swirling mist,' exclaimed Laura, inspired, as she craned her head to look up the embankment upon which there had once been railway lines. At any rate, ghost train or no, she was determined to have at least one swirling mist upon her holiday.

'Perhaps the ghost train would take you away on it and never come back again,' Andrew had said in a hopeful, brotherly voice.

Laura was a discontented enthusiast. That is, she was so often all set for really interesting things to happen and they so rarely ever did that she found herself constantly cheated and disappointed. She felt that, through no fault of her own, her life lacked drama: on a day of high wind and racing cloud when every sense tingled, for instance, it was, it *must* be all wrong merely to return home tamely for tea. She needed at such times to leap bareback on to a horse, twist her hands into its flowing mane, whisper into its ear (they were always doing that in the kind of books she read: historical, adventure *or* pony) and gallop off daringly somewhere across country through flood, fire and earthquake to bring important news, escape her enemies or save someone's life. She was sure she would be good at that. But the opportunity never seemed to come.

And so they had arrived. After their first, hurried exploration, Andrew and Laura bore their respective suitcases up to their respective rooms. They were given two clean sheets and a pillow case each by their mother and told to make up their beds with the blankets they would find already folded upon them. Andrew could be seen through the open door of his room methodically unpacking. Laura struggled up the five steps to her room, dumped the suitcase on the bed, dropped the sheets on the floor and forgot about them. Now she had time to notice that her room was all green: green linoleum, greenish rag mat which skated about the floor whenever you kicked it, green striped wallpaper, which was hanging loose in a great fold behind the door. There was no cupboard, but a curtained-in corner with somebody's very old mackintosh hanging on it. There was a little hardbacked chair by the bed. There was one small chest of drawers with a spotted mirror hanging above.

'Mirror, mirror on the wall, who is the ugliest girl of all?' Laura dramatically declaimed to it. She did not like her face. It remained silent, merely reflecting back a good deal of her long, curly hair, her eyes which she would have liked to be smoulderingly dark and huge and romantic and which were in fact small and blue, and a dirty mark down one side of her nose. Laura checked that the hair and eyes were as usual, but did not notice the dirty mark.

She had a sudden inspiration. What the room needed, of course, as it was all green, was yet more green. She would drown in greenness; it would be like living in a forest pool. What flowers were green? Green flowers ... There weren't any green flowers. All right, then – grasses, reeds. She would have an enormous pot of different grasses here, a smaller one there. She walked to and fro across the room as she visualized it, stepping over and sometimes tripping over the sheets on the floor as she did so. And perhaps one brilliant splash of red or white *here*.

In the meantime Andrew had gone to the bathroom and was washing some of the grime of the journey off his face and hands. He was a very clean boy: two years younger than Laura and a good deal smaller, though there were signs (the size of his feet for instance) that this state of affairs would not last so very much longer.

'I'm going out again,' cried Laura, who had forgotten all about washing, and clattered down the stairs. 'I simply must explore the outside properly, to see what grasses there are, and to look in the stables. I say, I wonder if William is a pony after all? Wouldn't that be simply great?'

She disappeared along the flagstone path that ran the length of the house, and though her voice drifted back at intervals nobody could hear what she was saying. This wasn't the sort of thing to stop Laura in full spate, however: she didn't always expect an audience.

But then, suddenly, she was back at the front door to meet her mother and Andrew at the foot of the stairs.

'I *say*,' she said in a hushed self-conscious voice very different from her usual cheerful, ringing tones, 'did you know we don't have this place to ourselves? There's a funny old man living above the stables: I saw a chimney smoking and he put his head out and looked at me and said something. Mrs Anderson didn't write anything about *him*, did she? Or do you think he could be William?'

# two

A strange old man in the stable. Here indeed was a slight mystery right away, but not one upon which Laura felt disposed to exercise any of her fertile imagination. Her mother was of much the same mind.

'I say, I really do think that is a bit thick,' she said in an irritated voice, on coming back from a quick peep on her own account. 'I mean one simply does *not* let a holiday cottage as empty when there is some hanger-on or aged retainer or what not living in one half of it: even if it is separate from the house we will be entirely overlooked. It is *not* the same as complete privacy and being on one's own, which was the very purpose of this holiday. We get overlooked enough in London. I *do* think Mrs Anderson might have made the position perfectly clear ... Lay the table for me, Laura, there's a good girl and quick about it. You'll find cutlery in that drawer, there. Andrew, you can find a tablecloth or mats or something somewhere. There must be something or other to put on a table. And there's not room in the kitchen, we'll have to eat on the table in the living room. Do hurry up, children, can't you see I'm nearly ready to dish up?'

Over the supper table, eggs and bacon and tea and cake (all of which things Mrs Hearst had brought down in a big carton of groceries) they began to forget their first annoyance and accept the old man's presence.

'I suppose we ought to go and say hello to him,' said Mrs Hearst at last, more pacifically, sipping her tea thoughtfully. 'I suppose he acts as a kind of caretaker, though come to think of it it's funny he didn't come to welcome us. Perhaps it was he who put the key in the door.'

'I don't expect he'll be any bother to us,' said Mr Hearst. 'We're the ones that'll make all the noise, after all.'

'Do you think he could possibly be William?' asked Andrew. 'And what do we feed him on, I wonder?'

'Oh no, surely not; I'm not expected to *feed* this old man on my holidays,' exclaimed his mother in horror.

'For heavens sake no: William must be a cat or a donkey or something,' said Mr Hearst.

'A donkey!' cried Laura, brightening, then relapsed again. 'There's no sign of one anywhere in a field and the stable's already occupied . . . Oh I wish it had been a pony and not an old man! An old man is so *boring*. Mummy, why can't you ring Mrs Anderson up and ask her what she means about William? And about the old man? Surely that's the way to find out?'

'Alas, I can't,' replied Mrs Hearst regretfully. 'Though I'd dearly like to. But Mrs Anderson is abroad now. She's a very busy woman, I understand, full of plans and good works and bustlings about of various kinds. I think she does have a reputation for being rather absent-minded, come to think of it. I expect she thinks she's told me everything already in the four letters I've had from her. But she obviously hasn't.'

'Let's explore a bit more and find the lake, which should only be down the road, and chat up this old chap before the light goes,' said Mr Hearst, getting up briskly.

The bottom part of the stable, where Laura had hoped to find a horse, was shut and bolted: it was the loft above, up the stone steps, that seemed to be inhabited. There was a wooden door to this loft, in two halves, like a stable door, the top half of which was slightly open. A smell of tobacco and wood smoke came from within.

'In fact, it's a byre rather than a stable, you know,' said Mr Hearst as they approached. 'Cows rather than horses would have been kept here.'

'Even cows would have been more interesting than an—' Laura's voice died away as she and her father and brother came to a halt among the nettles at the bottom of the steps while Mrs Hearst firmly mounted them, showing her usual determination to get to grips with whatever problem lay ahead of her.

Laura and Andrew saw a grey head just showing through: heard a few muffled replies to their mother's questions and then the top half of the door was slammed shut and she descended the steps, looking rather pink.

'I'm not sure he really understood me,' she said doubtfully. 'And his accent was very thick so I'm not sure if I understood him either. But what I think he said was not to bother him and he wouldn't bother us. I asked who William was and he just shook his head. He doesn't seem very agreeable.'

'The obvious thing to do is to ignore him,' said Mr Hearst sensibly. 'Come on, let's find that lake. It must be just over the brow of the hill and down the other side.'

It was. It was a beautiful lake set at the bottom of the valley with lush meadows on either side, creamy-white with meadow-sweet and pink and purple with ragged robin and marsh orchids. On the far side were reeds and thickets and a farm and then nothing but the lonely hills. The nearer side of the lake was more populated; there were two or three cars parked at the shingle verge and some caravans dotted about, a sailing boat with a red sail was just coming in to its mooring. The voices of the people aboard floated up to them, although they were really some distance away.

The sky was blue and cloudless now, and the setting sun shone on one side of the lake only: the other was in shadow. After the confinement of London, where buildings press about one so closely, there was the feeling of limitless space, of hill and moor rolling on for miles and miles, perhaps for ever.

'We'll go up in the hills tomorrow,' said Mr Hearst. 'I believe there's a Roman road somewhere up there, and some old lead mines.'

'Lead mines!' exclaimed Laura, revelling in the ancient feel of the words. 'That's it, Andrew. That's it! That's where our adventures begin. Down the lead mines!'

'Oh no, Laura, you're not going down any nasty mines. Anyway I expect they've all fallen in,' said her mother swiftly. 'We'll go up all together and have a look at them if you like. And there's something you've missed. Do you see the notice over on that farmhouse halfway down the road, towards the lake: what does it say?'

' "Pony trekking",' read out Laura in ecstasy. 'Oh *heaven,* oh joy! Mummy we *must* go pony trekking *and* see the lead mines. Oh Andrew, oh Mummy, oh Daddy I just *know* there'll be something terrific on this holiday about lead mines and ponies – there's got to be!'

'You, falling off a pony down a lead mine, I expect,' said Andrew. 'And you needn't expect me to pull you out, either.'

This kind of sneer from a young brother must be instantly resisted.

'Well, listen to you talking. And who was it that actually fell off a pony, you or me? Why, you even fell off that donkey on the sands the year before last.'

'Laura! Andrew!' put in their mother swiftly. 'Come on, let's go back, there's a lot of unpacking yet to do, the beds to make up if you haven't already done so, and it's been a long day.'

It had been a long day and the sun was very low. In silence they walked back over the brow of the hill and through the gate to Ramshead Lodge. About a quarter of a mile up the lane stood the farm which now owned all the pasture land around them and from which they would get their milk and eggs. There were no other houses in view. A goose, followed solemnly by five goslings, marched through the adjoining field towards a little stone hut at one end, otherwise nothing moved but the tops of the long grasses in the wind.

Laura walked in a dream; she imagined being up on the high moors above the fields; the lead mines. Swart men digging, the clank of spade upon stone, a tall moustached-and-booted man with a whip, upon a black horse, urging them on . . . something – a treasure? A dead body? – brought out muffled in a sack . . . it was all hundreds of years ago . . . but she saw it.

'Look, there's that old man,' exclaimed Andrew suddenly. 'Standing at the top of the steps.'

They all saw him for a moment, as he stood motionless, staring at them. He wore an old, fawn-coloured mackintosh, his grey hair blowing about his forehead. Then he turned and went back into his loft. In silence the Hearst family went down the track to the house. It was colder and darker than ever inside. Their thoughts turned towards the comfort of hot baths and bed.

Some hours later Laura woke from a muddled dream of ponies: she was on a pony but it was so small that her legs touched the ground on either side and she was still walking . . . to the dim realization that there was a noise going on somewhere. She sat up in bed. There was no bedside light and she did not feel like going to the light switch beside the door. It was very dark: although she had only partially drawn her curtains, hardly any light came from outside. There was the sound again; a low buzzing. No. Someone was *laughing*. It came from the wall beyond her room: through that wall was the loft where the old man lived. He was laughing alone; there were no other voices. He was laughing to himself, in a low voice on and on. Occasionally there was silence of perhaps a minute's duration and then he started again.

'I'm not frightened, but I don't like it,' Laura told herself. She wished she were sharing a room with Andrew. She wished she had not been so quick in seizing this particular room, off on its own at the end of the house.

It would be comforting if someone else heard the laughter. So Laura got out of bed and went down the corridor to Andrew's room. It took a little time to wake him, and once woken he was not as particularly keen to investigate midnight laughter as Laura would have wished.

'Please *do* come,' she was reduced to begging. 'I'll give you two pence – *five* pence if you like, only come.'

'Oh, all right.'

Her room looked bare and uncomfortable under the single light, hanging without a shade in the middle of the room. Her bedclothes had slipped mostly on to the floor.

'Can't hear anything,' said Andrew, scratching his head.

They listened together. There was complete, thick silence. Outside the black night pressed about them. Andrew yawned and turned to go back to his room. 'You must have dreamt it,' he said.

'I'm sure I didn't. I was dreaming about ponies,' said Laura, half-doubtfully. She couldn't have dreamt anything so definite as laughter – could she? And it lasted such a long time.

'Oh, you and your ponies! I'm going back to bed. You can come and sleep on the extra bed in my room if you're scared. But I thought you *liked* this room.'

'I did,' said Laura helplessly. She got into bed, leaving the light on. 'I shall sit up and listen all night and if he starts again I won't stay here another moment longer.'

The silence continued. Laura sat up for about half an hour. There was an owl. There was a dog barking. Then the silence yielded to the slight sound of snoring, for Laura was apt to snore when asleep on her back . . .

three

Andrew was awakened by the sound of voices. He put his head out of the window and there, just below him, stood a youth of about eighteen and a girl of Laura's age. The girl was broad rather than fat, with one thick brown plait, and wearing a cotton dress and boots to protect her legs from the wet grass.

'We've brought your milk,' she said. The milk was in an old-fashioned milk churn at her side. 'And mother says do you want any eggs?'

By now Laura was also awake and looking out of the window and she and Andrew ran downstairs for a few minutes' chat. The girl had slight possibilities, Laura decided. They must indeed be much the same age. A ginger cat suddenly appeared, yowling vigorously and wrapping himself round everybody's legs.

Andrew was inspired.

'Is this cat William?' he asked.

'Aye.'

'We were told to feed him if we see him.'

'Ah well, you see sometimes he lives with us and sometimes here,' said the girl from the farm. 'And sometimes nowhere; he's off hunting for weeks at a time.'

There was one mystery cleared up at any rate. William continued to express his extreme willingness to be fed by anyone.

'And the old man in the loft,' said Laura. 'Do you know anything about him? Has he always lived there? You see he was rather a surprise to us. Mrs Anderson didn't mention him at all.'

'Naw – we don't know of *him*,' said the youth. 'I've not seen an old man around here. Mrs Anderson has all sorts at times though – students and the like. We don't reckon to know everybody that's here. They come and go, you see.'

'If he's here he don't get milk from us anyway,' added his sister.

They all looked in the direction of the loft. It was shut and there was no sign of life.

'Funny,' said Laura, dubiously. She became aware that she was wearing only her pyjamas.

'Well, goodbye,' she said, retreating modestly behind the door.

'Goodbye. You'll come up when you want more milk then?'

The girls exchanged one more penetrating glance at one another, and then the two from the farm went on their way. Laura closed the door and found the cat already inside, running before her expectantly into the kitchen.

'Mummy!' she called upstairs. 'Mummy, are you up yet? William is a cat and wants his breakfast. What can I feed him on besides milk? Can we buy some cat food for him?'

She forgot the old man: she forgot the strange laughter in the night which she had obviously dreamt. It was going to be a lovely day, and they had pony trekking and hills and a lake before them: not to mention a very hungry, friendly and vocal cat who needed instant attention.

A warrior from Ghengis Khan's army swept down the mountainside on his sure-footed hill pony. He flourished his sword in the air, twirled his long moustaches, then reined his panting mount in, waiting for the rest of the golden horde to catch him up, before they mustered for the final assault on – on – Samarkand or Tashkent, or one of those places.

Laura's pony resisted all her attempts to stop him from eating grass. She let the reins drop on his fat woolly neck and waited for the other four pony trekkers to catch her up. Andrew was last.

'Did you see the old man?' he asked. 'Back on the top, near the tarn.'

'No, what old man?'

'Don't be silly. Our old man, the one who scared you by laughing last night.'

'Oh,' said Laura, bringing herself back from her dream of Tartar warriors. 'No, I didn't.'

The scary feeling of last night was quite gone, here, coming down from the many-coloured moors where the birds had called and the sun had shone and one saw immeasurable blue distances over the wide world.

'He was standing leaning on a kind of crook, q looking at us.'

'I never saw him,' said Laura again.

'I want to speak to him,' said Andrew rather une pectedly.

'Why on earth?'

'I don't know. I just do.'

'What do you want to say, for heaven's sake?'

'It's not that I want to say anything exactly, it's just that I want to speak with him.'

Laura made a face and turned her attention to hauling up her pony's head and kicking him onwards.

That evening Andrew and Laura washed up the supper things while their parents walked up the lane for a stroll.

It was getting late but the sun was out and it was still very light. It was impossible to remain indoors after the last plate had been dried and put away, so they went out. The shadows of trees and of the house were long and slanting across the grass. The light was gold and green.

'What shall we do?'

'I don't know. Don't ask me.'

'Let's play something.'

'*Play* something?' he queried, as if play were something he never did. 'Play what?'

They wandered about, kicking at the tussocks of grass.

'Here's an old tennis ball,' exclaimed Laura, picking it up. 'Come on, Andrew, let's play french cricket. Use that piece of wood for a bat.'

'Girls don't hit hard enough to make cricket worthwhile,' returned Andrew loftily. Nevertheless he picked up the piece of wood and lashed out with it as Laura threw the ball at his legs.

'Can't catch either,' he taunted her infuriatingly as she missed an easy one, the sun being in her eyes.

'Right. I'm going to get you now, Andrew Hearst.' She rolled up her sleeves with a flourish.

'No, you're not, oh no you're not,' he crowed cockily. He

21

and enjoy himself. 'Watch out, here it

the ball with a confident, cricketer's stance,
y so that it sped past and lost itself in the
nettles near the stables. Laura, retrieving,
looked up, and there the old man was, standing at the top of
the stable steps.

'Good evening to you,' he said.

'Good evening,' she replied politely, but she was a little
startled.

He looked and sounded different from the shabby old
man who had mumbled to her mother the previous day, his
face seemed pinker and smoother, his voice more precise.

'I was wondering if you and your brother would like to
come up and have a look round my little place?'

'Well, er—' began Laura doubtfully. She had been enjoying the game, they didn't often play together nowadays. At
home Andrew was usually involved with a crowd of his
friends and didn't want her. But Andrew, instantly and
without hesitation, said, 'Yes, please.'

And so, because Laura could find no good reason not to,
they climbed up the stable steps.

Once inside, they found they had been even more mistaken in their idea of the kind of place he was living in. For
the room before them was not in the least like a stable loft. It
had a rich carpet upon the floor and was profusely and ele-
gantly furnished: in fact it was not unlike the inside of an
antique shop, of the kind that goes in for a great many
interesting and valuable little objects set about on the tops
of chests and occasional tables and writing desks. There was
also a small fireplace with a small basket grate and mantelpiece above and before it a table set with a pretty china
teaset, three teacups, silver teaspoons and a bowl of lump
sugar and a jug of milk, just as if he had been expecting
them.

Andrew and Laura instantly felt all large, clumsy body
and awkward knocking hands and feet. It was, however, just

possible to pick a way to the tea table to which they were summoned.

'Now I do hope you'll take a cup of tea with me. I always find it a very soothing drink when I'm making new friends. And the boy is Andrew and the girl is Laura. You see I know all about you.'

He had taken his old mackintosh off and his underneath clothes made them revise their first impressions of him even more rapidly. He was wearing a black, polo-neck jersey of fine soft wool, and beneath it impeccably-creased grey flannel trousers. He had expensive-looking black suéde slippers on his feet. Now they were near him they could see too the smoothness of his well-shaven cheeks, the cultivation of his wavy grey hair, worn fashionably long like a young man's so that it covered the bottom of his ears. He could not be much over sixty, if that.

'Now, we'll have Laura just here by the little china cherub clock – note the cherubs are holding it and their expressions – and Andrew over here, my dear, facing the window, that's right. You can have this pedestal table for your cup. Do you take sugar?'

'One lump please,' said Andrew carefully. Laura could see he was wearing his very-interested expression. For her part she simply felt very surprised, puzzled and just slightly resistant. She wasn't in the mood for polite conversation; besides, it was odd, why did he live like this; why was he making up to them?

Now he was showing Andrew a little decorated snuffbox.

'Because I see you're a young gentleman of discernment. You appreciate good quality.'

'You have some beautiful things,' said Andrew eagerly.

'Thank you. I flatter myself that during a long life of collecting I've managed to acquire a few pieces of some artistic merit. I never thought I would come to make my home up here so far from civilization, but it has its advantages, it has its advantages. One can gather all one's things about one and make a little island of culture.'

'Oh yes,' said Laura politely. She still felt uneasy and cast about for a reason for them to leave. 'I wonder if our parents will be back now and wondering what is happening to us?'

'They were going out for half an hour at least and only a quarter has gone by.' Andrew had obviously no intention of budging and held up his wrist for her to see his wrist watch.

Bother Andrew, bother his watch which he always wore and which always kept good time, unlike Laura's watch which she forgot to wind, forgot to put on, forgot the whereabouts of.

'We might take a little stroll presently ourselves,' said the old man, smiling at Laura.

His eyes were very round and blue and innocent-looking; his smile showed perfect, if slightly yellowing teeth.

Laura drank some of her tea: it had a fragrant, smoky taste. She wondered if it were china tea which she had not previously tasted. She watched a very small spider climb the edge of the table, pause, and then slowly let itself down and out of sight on an invisible thread. It hadn't spun a web: it was the kind of small spider one didn't associate with large webs and flies sticking in them, so why did the opening lines of this song suddenly come into her head:

'Will you come into my parlour, said the spider to the fly,
'Tis the prettiest little parlour that ever you did spy.'

But she and Andrew had not given the right reply:

'Not today thanks Mr Longshanks,
 We've other fish to fry.'

They had gone in and – what was she thinking of? She was letting her imagination run away with her as it always did: it wasn't like that – he was only a smallish, slightly-built elderly man. Why, she, Laura, would be well past his shoulder if they stood up, and Andrew was very strong for his age.

Again, what was she thinking: if they stood up? They *were* standing up; they were going to stroll down towards the lake to see the sun set; it had been spoken of as a sight worth seeing.

'Please sir,' said Andrew, in his politest prep-school voice as he carefully manoeuvred his way to the door, 'what are we to call you? What is your name?'

The old man paused as he threw something dark about his shoulders, not his mackintosh, a cape or cloak.

'That is a very good question. I had forgotten that as far as names went I had the advantage of you. I should think you had better call me Mr Strange. Yes, that would be very nice. Mind the steps, there's a broken one. I'm afraid the outside of my little home is in shocking condition.'

Laura followed, shaking her head to try and clear it as they came out into the fresh, cool air. Why hadn't he simply said 'My name is Mr Strange', instead of 'I think you had better call me Mr Strange'? Why did she feel suspicious of him and why was she feeling queer, slowed-up, confused, as if everything were going too fast for her? She was getting left behind. Andrew, pale, intent, was walking pace for pace with him and was hanging on his every word. They were speaking of fishing, of fish, of – Laura stumbled over her feet as she tried to catch them up.

Fish; creatures moving dimly through dark, quiet waters . . . It was at this point, as they took the turning down the hill towards the lake, that the world changed.

First the noises. Their footsteps, which had been loud, sharp on the hard surface of the road became deadened, muffled and then the sound of their walking ceased altogether. But they were still descending the hill, Mr Strange first, his cape lifting gently behind him, Andrew at his heels, Laura a pace or so behind. No sound of their feet, no birds, no wind, no car or boat engines, but a soft, soft silence. There must be a mist rising from the lake a hundred or so yards beneath them because it became harder to see it, the reeds and rushes at the edge had gone from view; it became difficult even to see their soundless feet.

As if a lens had been turned and focused before her eyes

to give her a different outlook, Laura began to see both more dimly and yet with more piercing clarity than she had ever seen in her life before. All trace of self-conscious awareness of herself as a girl called Laura, shrivelled, dropped away like a dead skin: anything could happen now. She was beginning to find she could see *through* things; that although a mist muffled the outer edges of objects about her, she could see under a rock they had just passed to the scurrying insects beneath it. There was a grass snake motionless at the roots of the long grass. She could see through the grass to see it. She was becoming more and more aware of small furry and feathery bodies crouched in holes and nests and hollows in the fields about them, of bright eyes that watched and peered and blinked. Down they still went, soundlessly, until they stood upon the shore of the lake.

A car was being loaded up by the gravel beach that bordered the road side of the lake: the last car of the day. A boat stood neatly in a trailer, the children who together with their parents had been out in it on the water were just climbing into the car. The eyes of the youngest child, a boy of about six, flicked incuriously past Laura as if he did not know she was there. The car moved away on silent wheels and there was no sound of its engine.

It was their last contact with the everyday world. She didn't turn to watch it go because of what she now began to see through the surface of the lake. Close under or just breaking the skin of the water roamed little things, insects and small fish, but further towards the centre, deeper down, Laura realized there were bigger shapes. Huge fish moved sluggishly, eel-like creatures writhed, and if she paused and waited she had the most curious sensation that she would be able to see the world through their eyes: there was a feeling of a kind there, and almost thought. Through these creatures she became aware of other creatures, in other lakes and lochs, in the deeps of the sea itself, she felt a kind of understanding of them grow, she felt—

'Stand just here, Laura,' came Mr Strange's voice gently behind her. 'And Andrew here. That's very good.'

They had come to a halt at the very edge of the water, by a rock. The sun cut across the far hills on the other side of the lake; only a slice of it was left, it was going and as it went and the colour and brightness went with it the enchantment bit deeper and Laura realized there were other presences about her, farther now from any reality she had known. There were eyes, there were faces looking at her from the trees to the west of the lake: sad faces, gloating, malign faces, inward-looking, self-absorbed faces, ruddy, coarse faces, faces with hair and fur. Beast and human now were mixing, melting into one another, great bodies moved slowly far beyond the trees, high on the moors, and she didn't know if they were human or animal. Something, someone other than human was near a waterfall deep in a winding valley, and from the top of the farthest hill, within a high cliff edge, they were again watched: there was a powerful, brooding stone face, a shrouded something with reaching fingers of rock that became aware of her and of Andrew and twitched and moved within the rock. Then as the last trace of brightness from the vanished sun faded from the sky, Laura felt hard cold fingers seize her arm and a cry, not gentle, mellifluous as his voice had been, but harsh, exultant, rang out and echoed in her ears:

'I have you! I have you!'

Laura was just able to croak out a desperate 'No! Not me!' when everything swam about her, her knees gave way, a mist came up right inside her head and she saw and remembered no more.

# four

Laura woke slowly the next morning: she felt extremely tired and full of sleep: at last a noise penetrated: her mother's voice. She had come into the room where Laura and Andrew now slept together and was drawing the curtains.

'Well, we *have* all slept late this morning,' she said, letting in a stream of sunlight. 'It must be the country air. Breakfast is nearly ready, so you can come down in your pyjamas and dressing gowns if you like.'

'I didn't bring my dressing gown,' mumbled Laura. 'I'll put my clothes on.'

As she was dressing she struggled to remember the events of the evening before. Slowly they arranged themselves in her mind but she had no memory of returning to the house and of going to bed: yet they had obviously done so, and in an ordinary, unnoticeable way or her mother would not have been so brisk and matter-of-fact. But what exactly had happened? Had she been unwell, or drugged in some way, had Andrew? A thrill of unease went through her as she watched him methodically putting on his trousers. In some indefinable way he didn't look quite right: he hadn't spoken, he hadn't yawned or gone to the window, he had simply arisen and was dressing.

'It's going to be a good day again,' she remarked, hoping that ordinary, dull conversation would prove her mistaken.

He glanced at the window but made no reply. His face was smooth, expressionless.

'Did you enjoy the walk with Mr Strange last night? I had such a peculiar sort of dream after it,' Laura said, sitting down beside him on the bed, her unease growing. Indeed, *had* it been a dream? Could she ever see such things again?

Andrew paused and looked at her. Something moved far

back in his eyes. But he made no reply. He went over to the mirror and brushed his hair.

'Andrew, are you all right?'

He went on brushing his hair.

'I mean, do you feel all right after last night? Do you remember going to bed?'

He put the brush down. He did not look at her.

'Oh, I do wish you'd answer me; it's dreadfully rude not to answer people when they speak to you, you know,' scolded Laura, worry growing and growing in her mind as moment after moment went by and he did not respond. She was now convinced that something had changed him. He turned, to try and pass her to leave the room, but she stood in the doorway and barred his passage.

'You're going to speak to me,' she cried passionately. '*Please* Andrew, you've got me all worried. Please be all right.'

'Do you mind?' he said icily, after a moment's standing before her. His eyes, hostile, looked past her. 'I want to get to the bathroom.'

'But why didn't you *answer* me?'

'There is nothing to say.'

The cold, precise dislike in his voice left Laura speechless, and she let him push past her and walk down the passage to the bathroom. The door shut and was locked.

'All right, *be* like that then,' said Laura to the empty bedroom. But she knew something was dreadfully wrong.

At breakfast he was better, in that he answered his parents' remarks and questions, but he still made no observation of his own. Laura tried to forget him, to concentrate on her own breakfast, but she could not. She could have screamed at the unawareness of her parents; he was so changed, but they saw nothing. Why, the very way he held his knife and fork, the way he methodically cut up his fried bread into little squares and speared them one by one with his fork was different: he never usually ate like that.

After breakfast Andrew and Laura washed up without speaking to one another. Andrew went upstairs and Laura followed him.

'What are you going to do?' she tried, but did not get an answer.

He made his bed neatly and then lay upon it, staring at the ceiling.

'Andrew, please, please listen to me and answer me. I want to know what happened to us down at that lake last night. I feel all right now, except for the dreams, but what about you? If you're not feeling right we'll tell Mummy and Daddy. We'll get someone to do something about it.'

He turned his head and looked at her then. 'We won't,' he said. 'Leave me alone.'

'But I *can't* leave you alone!'

And now he did not answer her.

'Oh!' cried Laura desperately, stamping her foot. 'I was only trying to help. Why are you like that to me? It's as if you hated me all of a sudden. What have I done wrong?'

'Just leave me alone.'

'All right, I *will.*'

She tossed her bedclothes wildly back on to her bed and dashed out of the room. Downstairs she found her mother organizing her father into taking the car and buying some groceries and meat. Later they would all go for a walk and a picnic.

'Want to come with me?' asked her father.

'No, thank you. I'm going outside.'

Laura opened the gate for her father to drive out and then wandered restlessly in the meadow before the house. And she saw Mr Strange, looking trim and elegant in his black polo-necked jersey, come out on to the top of his steps and look at her. As he did so Andrew came out of the front door and walked towards them.

'Ah, good morning Laura, good morning Andrew. And how are you both this lovely day?'

This innocent-sounding question sounded most ominously in Laura's ears. Andrew pushed past her to stand below Mr Strange at the foot of the steps.

'Very well, thank you,' he said.

He said it like an automaton, a puppet, as if someone were manipulating his strings. The way he said it gave Laura a dreadful pang and she cried out: 'He isn't well, Mr Strange, and I had terrible dreams. What did you do to us, what did you do to him, what has happened?'

Mr Strange looked at her and an expression of annoyance came over his face. He picked his way delicately down the few broken steps to stand beside them and gaze carefully into their faces, first Andrew, then Laura. After he had looked at Laura he sighed and said:

'Oh dear yes, I can see, it's hardly taken at all, how disappointing. You must be a very thick-headed, insensitive subject, Laura.'

He waved his hands rapidly over her face, inadvertently brushing her nose with his little finger as he did so.

'Don't do that. Ow!' said Laura, flinching and stepping backwards.

Meanwhile Mr Strange was making the same movements over Andrew's face. Andrew merely looked at him attentively without blinking his eyes.

'Oh well, the boy is in nice and deep, anyway. A most satisfactory little piece of enchantment,' announced Mr Strange, as if to himself.

'Whatever do you mean, *enchantment*?' cried Laura fearfully. It was true: her worst suspicions were confirmed, and yet she could hardly believe it. Enchantment sounded so old-fashioned, so odd, like a fairy story.

'You shouldn't have done it. Did you put something in the tea? I shall tell Mummy. I shall tell Daddy. You're not allowed to go about doing that kind of thing!'

'My dear Laura, of course I didn't put anything in the tea. I wouldn't spoil a good cup of china tea like that. What a song and dance you do make. And you will find it quite impossible telling your parents anything, do give me the credit of a little experience.' He bent down and peered into the motionless Andrew's face again. 'A lovely little piece of work,' he said, with a satisfied expression. 'Of course he was a good subject.'

'But you didn't get me!' Laura cried. 'All I had was dreams – or something.' She could say this, in the confident morning light, but it had been more than dreams and she knew it. He had had some effect on her; she had not been able to resist him entirely.

'No,' agreed Mr Strange, with an air of great reasonableness and civility, 'I did not, as you say, get you. There are some few, very unimaginative and thick-headed and thick-souled people who are not capable of being touched deeply by my art. You must be one of them.'

'But – but—' Laura was torn by conflicting emotions: finally incredulous vanity triumphed. Why, *she* had always been the imaginative one, it was she who wrote stories and poetry and read heaps of books: of *her* Miss Hartley, her English teacher, had said: 'Laura has a fine flow of imaginative and creative feeling.' Imagination was her *thing*, her forte; it was not Andrew's who, when he read at all, read books on aeroplanes and trains and astronomy and football. You couldn't call that kind of reading imaginative. It wasn't really proper reading at all. Thick-headed, thick-souled! Laura had never been so insulted in her life. The insult woke in her a very healthy strain of courageous resistance to Mr Strange and dislike of him: she was not going to let him get away with it. Besides, Andrew could not be allowed to continue in this state. Mr Strange must unenchant him, *immediately*. She supposed it was really some kind of advanced hypnosis he had practised on Andrew. He was trying to kid her with this word enchantment, as though she were a young child who believed in such stuff.

'You've hypnotized him then,' she cried angrily. 'You didn't get me because I was suspicious and resisted you. That's what's happened. I read somewhere that you can't be hypnotized against your will.'

'Please don't shout at me,' said Mr Strange mildly. 'And I dislike standing arguing like this. Why don't we all go up the steps and into my little place and sit down comfortably, like reasonable beings?'

Andrew made an instant movement towards the steps and Laura caught his arm and held him.

'No!' she said. 'We are not going into that room of yours again!'

'Very well,' replied Mr Strange, his eyes round, innocent, reasonable, as if he were going out of his way to humour her. 'We will sit here on the steps.'

Andrew sat beside him but Laura was determined to do nothing he suggested and continued to stand.

'You say I hypnotized your brother. It just shows your ignorance, my poor girl. I would never interest myself in anything so utterly commonplace as hypnotism, nor is it done in the least like a proper enchantment: indeed it is a very poor, mechanical affair altogether.'

'Enchantment: you mean, then, like being bewitched? It is a kind of witchcraft?' asked Laura slowly and incredulously.

Thoughts of black witches and Masses ran through her head; *had* there been such people as witches, was there anything in it? She remembered a rather unsatisfactory programme on television about witches and the supernatural, which left one still guessing. Mr Strange drew back with a movement of disgust.

'Witchcraft, my dear girl, what can you be thinking of? I'm *nothing* like a witch, such a vulgar low-grade kind of person usually. That kind of behaviour is for the peasantry, all this falling about into fits and foaming at the mouth, sticking of pins into waxen images, cooking abominable messes with toads' entrails and newts' tongues (disgusting, disgusting!), sinking ducks and drying up cows' udders: all so *very* coarse and physical. I am a gentleman of birth and breeding: enchantment is a very high profession, a great art which has taken many centuries to perfect. *Witches* indeed –

but then I suppose, Laura, this is why you can't appreciate my enchantment. Your mind is only capable of working in one particular way on what I should call a very earthbound level.'

At this moment a dreadful thing happened: at least it seemed a dreadful thing to Laura. For her little brother Andrew, whom she had quarrelled with and played with and been exasperated with and yet loved, turned to her and looked at her and said the one word 'Earthbound' and the dull, lifeless yet entirely matter-of-fact way in which he said it made the word a more terrible word of abuse than Laura had ever heard from him before. 'Earthbound': it came out in a kind of croak and was infinitely wounding. Funny, round-headed, solemnly humorous Andrew had turned into something completely alien. He treated her as an enemy; worse, as if she were of an entirely different and lower species.

Then there was the sound of a car turning through the gate, their father returning from his shopping expedition, while at the same time their mother came out of the front door with a bowl full of washing to hang upon the line.

'I will say goodbye to you for the present,' said Mr Strange, rising and dusting down his trousers.

'But what about Andrew, what will happen to Andrew?' called Laura to him desperately as he opened the door to his room.

'Oh, Andrew. Yes. The enchantment must take its course, naturally.' He smiled brightly at her and shut the door.

'Andrew, Laura!' came their mother's voice. 'Come and get ready, we'll be off presently.'

'I must say something about Andrew to them. I can't handle this on my own,' thought Laura desperately. How could Mr Strange stop her telling her mother what had happened: he was surely boasting about this. She already had an idea that he was a man of no small conceit.

She found her mother in the kitchen, packing up the picnic basket.

34

'I'm worried about Andrew,' she began. She meant to continue, 'You see he's been enchanted', was sure there'd be no difficulty in getting the words out (for a moment she had wondered if Mr Strange could affect her tongue so it couldn't speak for her, but this was plainly ridiculous). Then she paused, realizing that her mother would simply stare unbelievingly at the word 'enchanted', so she changed her mind and went on rather lamely, 'I don't think he's very well.'

'Yes I am, perfectly well,' said Andrew, coming up just behind Laura. He looked well, too: pink cheeked, his eyes bright.

'Oh Laura darling, it's sweet of you, but really you needn't worry over Andrew,' said her mother, carefully pressing the sandwiches into a tin. 'You mustn't nanny him too much you know, darling. Boys don't like it. But you'd be a marvellous eldest sister to some much younger brothers and sisters, as I've said before.'

'She could boss them to her heart's content,' agreed Andrew. 'Have you remembered to put in some chocolate?' He said this very normally and Laura realized that her approach had been all wrong. If only it wasn't somehow rooted in her family's mind that she was an over-protective, bossy elder sister so that they didn't listen properly to her! She couldn't think *why* she was thought of like this, but knew she was.

And so they set off on their picnic and walked and walked on a track that took them past the high fields with stone walls around them to the open moor above and at last to a stone cairn that marked the top of the nearest of the hills. They found a good place out of the wind and their mother distributed egg sandwiches while their father spread out a map.

'I'd just like to get myself orientated,' he said. 'It's so confusing lower down because there are valleys and hidden shoulders of land one never sees, but it ought to be simple enough up here. You can't quite see Ramshead Lodge but look, that must be the clump of trees behind the farm. Then taking the far side of the lake from here you go up that line of trees – see, Laura? – and come to Ramshead Gill, a stream; higher up there are a couple of waterfalls marked, and the highest is called Ramshead Force. Do you see on the map?'

'I *think* so,' said Laura, confused by squiggly contour lines.

Andrew said nothing but chewed on a pork pie. High on this open moor with so much country to see, mile upon mile of it and the sun out and eating egg sandwiches and pies, why, it was impossible, Laura thought, that anything was other than normal and cheerful. It was hot in the sun, and the heather and short grass smelt agreeably. The enchantment, or whatever it had been, was wearing off: Mr Strange had been laughing at them. Everything would be normal now.

'Above Ramshead Force must be this large area marked Firedale Forest,' continued Mr Hearst, between bites of his sandwich.

'See, Andrew, it's over that valley there, all the open moorland stretching along below High Scar Edge where those cliffs are. You can't see them so well from here. And this is Cobbler's Seat. We're sitting at the top of Cobbler's Seat.'

Andrew nodded.

'Why is it called Firedale Forest if there aren't any trees?' asked Laura. 'Forests should have trees.'

'There were trees a long time ago. But they were cut down and the sheep did for whatever others that tried to grow. These hills have been grazed and grazed by sheep for hundreds and hundreds of years.'

'Let me have the map please, Daddy,' Laura begged. It was hard to relate it to the countless hilltops about them, so she relaxed and just looked at the names.

High Scar Edge, Loudwater Force, Stonydale Moor, Mirky Bottom (that was a good one), Stony Head Pike, Cobbler's Seat . . .

Andrew ate milk chocolate. Laura ate milk chocolate and continued to look at the map until she was tired of it. There was something a little odd here . . . she couldn't quite think what. Then she realized. She had subconsciously been expecting Andrew to squabble with her for possession of the map, to give her about ten grudging seconds and then snatch it from her. It was all *wrong* that she should have been able to take her fill of it without a quarrel. Andrew loved maps. He drew beautiful ones for geography lessons at school and many more just for fun. And he simply lay back in the heather and looked at the sky.

'Do you want the map?' she asked. 'I've quite finished with it.'

'No,' he said quietly.

And then it was that Laura had the disquieting thought that, for whatever good reason, she had after all *not* succeeded in telling her parents of Andrew's difference or enchantment or whatever it was. She had tried, but she had failed. Mr Strange had said (what had he said?), he had said: 'You must give me the credit of having a little experience.'

And there were other words that lingered resonantly somewhere deeper in her memory and gave her yet greater unease: this unease that despite all rational thought lay deep within her. A curlew cried its plaintive bubbling cry somewhere from the moor below them and the words calmly spoke themselves again in Laura's mind: 'The enchantment must take its course.'

*The enchantment must take its course.*

# five

'Do hurry out of the bathroom, you've been ages,' Laura shouted through the keyhole.

Silence: earlier on there had been splashing, now there was silence.

'I want my bath!'

The silence remained unbroken. Suddenly Laura had a dreadful vision of him lying drowned under the water, flat on his back. It washed over his open mouth, his hair drifted in it. She forgot that the bath was a small one and that if Andrew's head were underneath, his knees must be bent or his feet out at the end. No, she saw him stretched out entirely, a naked corpse.

'Andrew!' she cried, and then, 'Mummy, oh Mummy, come quickly!'

There was the sound of someone getting out of a bath. Her mother and father were downstairs with the door shut and hadn't heard anyway. Quite quickly after that he unlocked the door and came out.

'Andrew, why are you so horrid? Can't you fight against whatever it is that Mr Strange has done to you? Can't you stop him from altering you?'

It was the first time she had spoken to him directly since their picnic lunch; all the rest of that day she had tried to ignore him, to ignore her worry: perhaps that was the way to make it go away. But her scare over the bath had loosened her resolve and she spoke without thinking, from the heart.

He tried to push by her without speaking, but she caught his pyjama'd arm.

'Do leave me alone,' he said, then, with cold dislike. 'What business is it of yours?'

'But what happens to you *is* my business,' said Laura. 'I'm your sister, and I'm older than you.'

It didn't seem a very good answer, even to her as she made it.

'You can't do anything,' he twitched his sleeve from her arm. 'You can't stop me.'

'Stop you from doing what?' called Laura after him. Her bath temporarily forgotten, she followed him into their room.

'Stop you from doing what?'

He got into bed, took out his miniature chess set, and set out the pieces.

'Oh, what's the *use*?' Laura slammed the door, but had to return after a few seconds for her pyjamas. He hunched over his chess problem, ignoring her.

Wallowing in her bath Laura resolved to let him be: to let them all be. If her parents didn't, *wouldn't* notice, and he continued like that, they could all just stew in their own juice. She would enjoy her holiday her own way. She determinedly began to read the book she had brought in with her.

Yet the very next day she could not help herself. She had to try again and tell one of her parents or she would burst.

Andrew had slept well. His sleeping and eating were good. But he awoke the next morning and this time before he got dressed he looked out of the window. He stood looking out of the window for half an hour with Laura doing her best to ignore him. At the call of breakfast he went downstairs naturally enough. After breakfast he went out into the meadow and stood by the gate. Laura watched him furtively despite all her better resolutions, and she saw Mr Strange come out on to his steps and instantly, although he was some distance away and had his back turned to him, Andrew swirled round and began to walk swiftly towards Mr Strange.

Laura could not endure them to meet alone. She was not frightened of Mr Strange, not she. A little, mild-spoken man like that! So she ran out of the house and stood near them. Andrew halted at the bottom of the steps, stood stiffly to attention and said nothing.

'Ah,' exclaimed Mr Strange benignly. 'A fine morning to

you both. Splendid, splendid. You're coming along very nicely, Andrew.'

And with these words he turned and went back into his loft.

Laura left Andrew sitting at the bottom of the steps. She ran inside to find her father. She had failed in trying to tell her mother; well, it was difficult to tell one's mother things sometimes. But her father, when he paid attention, often understood her better and was more sympathetic.

She found him alone in the dusty little parlour with pieces of his fishing rod about him and his fishing basket upon the table. He was tying flies, prior to a fishing expedition with Andrew that afternoon. Laura had forgotten this, although fishing these holidays by the two enthusiasts of the family had been much spoken of, and a fishing licence for a stretch of stream called Loudwater Beck obtained from the nearest village where they dispensed such things.

'Changed your mind? Like to come with us after all?' asked her father in a rather absent-minded voice as he concentrated on the tying of a fly. 'Rather fun this one, isn't he? He's called Greenwell's Glory.'

The brightly coloured artificial fly looked at Laura somehow although it had no face.

'I don't want to fish, thanks,' said Laura. 'You know what happened when I tried in Hampshire that time.' She had got soaked to the waist, stepping in the wrong place, and had got her line caught in a tree; she had felt so sorry for a fish caught by her father he had had to put it back. It had not been a success.

'I suppose Andrew does want to come,' she began carefully. She was determined to get it right this time, and not to say anything she did not mean or which could be taken the wrong way. 'He's behaving a little oddly at the moment.'

'Is he? I hadn't noticed. Damn!' He had dropped the fly.

'He won't talk to me,' said Laura. She was going to be able to say it after all. She would say it, straight out. 'You see he's fallen under the power of an enchanter.'

But unfortunately the last four words of her sentence were lost because the most overpowering cough came over her and she bent almost double, her eyes streaming.

'Oh dear.' Her father busily thumped her on the back. 'I thought for a moment you'd swallowed my fly, but here he is, quite safe and sound.'

Laura struggled a few minutes longer. 'He's fallen—' she gasped between bouts, 'he's en—'

'He's fallen in what? Better go and get a drink for that cough. Look, here he is. Whatever he fell in he got out of again. All right, Andrew, come here a minute. I want to show you how to tie a fly. You can do this one.'

Laura retreated from the room in disarray. The tears that ran down her face were as much from frustration as from the coughing fit. So he *could* affect her speech: if she tried to say the words directly she would cough, she would choke, it would not be any use. And her parents would make no effort to understand her. Although she half knew it was not their fault, she blamed them dreadfully. Her mother patronized her: her father laughed at her. That was what they were like. That was what they would always be like.

When Andrew and his father took up their rods and set off that afternoon Laura did not know what to do. Her mother carried out a kitchen chair, put it in a sunny place and settled down to read one of the detective stories she had brought with her, but Laura found it impossible to follow suit. She wandered restlessly in and out of the house several times and at last walked rapidly after the men. They were not very far away, along a deep stretch of the stream which led back through the dale towards the village where they did most of their shopping.

When she reached them they were already absorbed, Andrew standing on the bank, his father a little downstream and in the water. Watching them from the footpath some yards distant, Laura realized that another half-hope had gone, that Andrew on his own with his father was going to attract his attention by his odd behaviour. But this hope was unfounded: if Andrew was silent, if he stood for long periods together doing nothing much, it was totally unremarkable, because that is what fishing is like. She did not even call out to them: they presented such a calm and united masculine front against her intrusion.

So Laura looked at them hopelessly for a few minutes and then turned and walked back. They had not seen her. And all along the riverbank, beside the rushing sound of the water and the whispering leaves and in and out of shifting patterns of light and shade, she said out loud to herself to relieve her feelings:

'Andrew is enchanted, Andrew is enchanted,' and the water and the leaves at least listened and seemed to echo her words. The more she said the words out loud, the more she believed them.

And she knew that whatever happened, and however unpleasant Andrew was to her she must still persist in her efforts to save him. There was nothing else to do; she had no choice. There had never been any choice.

And so it was, upon the next day of her brother's enchantment, that Laura found herself sitting upon the stable steps having, for a few minutes, a further conversation with his enchanter. It had occurred to her that she had perhaps been rude and offended him earlier and that this was why he would not relax his mysterious hold over Andrew: if she were polite, if she pleaded with him, surely he would take pity on her and release her brother.

'You were quite right,' she said as she settled herself on the second step while Andrew stood beside her, his eyes fixed unwinkingly upon Mr Strange, 'you were perfectly right. I can't seem to find the words to tell Mummy and Daddy anything about what you've done to Andrew. He says nothing unless he's asked a question, he's never rude or silly or makes stupid jokes and yet they seem to think he is perfectly normal! I don't know how you've managed that, but you have and now, please Mr Strange, do you think, now that your experiment has worked so well, do you think you could possibly unenchant him, *please*?'

Mr Strange looked thoughtfully at Laura and then gave a little laugh.

'I don't know why you should think this is just a little *experiment*,' he said gently. 'I assure you there is nothing in the least experimental about my work. And I confess that I'm just a little amazed that you should think that because you say please do something which is contrary to all my desires and nature, I should do it! Of course I realize the world has changed a very great deal and people are a good deal more ignorant than they once were, but really, Laura, you do amuse me! Why, in the old days any rustic peasant youth or girl would at least have an inkling of what to do to undo an enchantment. They wouldn't waste much time in idle pleading, I assure you. I don't see why I should trouble myself to enlighten you, I don't indeed. Bless me, my dear Laura.' He began to laugh gently again and looked so very humorous and pleasant and indeed likeable that Laura did not altogether understand him; and pleaded again, with hope:

'Please undo the enchantment or whatever it is, Mr Strange, you're spoiling our holiday, and I'm sure it can't be very good for Andrew. He's not all that strong and he's growing so fast right now, and he always gets tonsillitis in the winter.'

Mr Strange looked at her, shaking with soft giggles, and said softly, 'But we're not going to wait until the winter. It's summer.'

'Summer or winter,' said poor Laura, confused, and tears not so very far away, 'please undo the enchantment, Mr Strange. I can't bear him as he is.'

'No, my ignorant twentieth-century girl, no indeed. The enchantment progresses. *I* am perfectly satisfied. And, dear me, what an unpleasant cloud that is over the sun. It has taken up quite half the sky. The weather is coming down today, thickening up, I don't think we shall have such a pretty day of it, indeed I don't. So if you'll excuse me, I shall turn back to the pleasures of my own fireside.'

Courteous as ever but his face totally unresponsive, blank to her, he turned up the steps and carefully latched the door upon them. Andrew instantly got up and walked back into the house, closing the front door so unseeingly behind him that it shut Laura out and nearly grazed her nose in the shutting. She stood in the first hard drops of rain, tears running down her face. It was the most desolating moment.

The clouds did indeed come down, the colours went from the hillsides, the hilltops disappeared altogether and everything was a dark greenish grey with the falling rain.

'I've found a store of firewood and logs,' said Mrs Hearst. 'They are in the bottom part of the stable beneath where the old man is living. Incidentally, I haven't seen him for a couple of days. At least he's quiet and unobtrusive. Anyway we'll have a fire and get all nice and cosy round it with our books, shall we?'

And so they did. The flames began to spurt merrily up and the wood crackled and smelt fragrantly.

'Like a game of chess, Andrew?' asked his father.

'No, thanks. I'm looking at these old magazines.'

Andrew stretched out on the rag mat with a 1936 copy of *Punch* he had found and remained motionless before it, staring at one page which he never turned. Laura, in desperation to avoid the sight of him so still, so unseeing, ferreted amongst the books in the bookcase in the parlour and found some children's stories: a very old-fashioned volume of boys' adventure stories, and a book of fairy tales.

She took the book of fairy stories; it was an Andrew Lang, the *Orange Fairy Book*; looked first at the beautifully detailed romantic illustrations and then settled down to read. It was peaceful reading like this, without having to bother with what was or was not on the television, because of course there was no television here. So while Andrew stared at one page of Fougasse drawings in *Punch*, Laura read first a story called 'The Two Caskets', then a story called 'The Girl Fish' and then a story called 'The Enchanted Wreath'. In many ways, she thought, these stories were absurd: it was hard to believe in a totally good sister and a totally bad sister, such as appeared in 'The Two Caskets' and 'The Enchanted Wreath' or in talking doves and fish ... and yet and yet ... The wicked sister in 'The Enchanted Wreath' as a punishment could only say 'dirty creatures': nothing else, however hard she tried. And now Laura could begin to understand this: how one could come not to have complete power over one's speech.

As she thought about these stories they seemed to sink deeper and deeper down into her and revived memories of when she had first read them years ago, when she was much younger, and of how her bedroom in which she had visualized them had looked (it was before it was decorated, when it still had a frieze of nursery animals round the walls), and somehow the look of these animals and her feeling about fairy stories and some of Mr Strange's remarks all mixed together with the sound of the rain outside and the crackle of the fire. 'You twentieth-century people,' Mr Strange had said. The world had changed, he had said, people were more ignorant, they had forgotten how to set about dealing with enchanters, just as she herself had almost forgotten the look of the animals round her bedroom walls.

As she paused and dreamed, even further-back memories floated back and she again saw her bedroom as it had once been, and now she remembered sitting on the bed in that room, sitting remembering back as she was now remembering back, seeing herself as an even smaller child. It was like looking at the reflection of a reflection in a mirror. This older memory, which had so nearly escaped her, came right up to her now: it was one of her first, she could only have been about three. She was in her parents' room, standing by their vast bed, looking up at her mother's huge dressing table. The surface where the brush and comb and powder pots lay was on a level with her head, and she was thinking calmly and rationally, 'What am I? Who am

I?' She remembered the pause at the end of this thought and then the peaceful realization: 'Why, I'm a little girl of course; that's what I am.'

What an odd little creature she must have been, hardly related to the Laura of nowadays and yet there was this continuous line of experience between them, and so she continued to plunge deep into other early dreams and memories and now she didn't know which was which, whether she was remembering things she had seen, or dreamt, or only been told about and imagined for herself. Far back within herself like this Laura felt her hold on reality slip; the reality of normal life and school and ponies, and now she had a sudden vision of a very different world underneath the normal. What if the fairy stories *really were true*? If there were still enchanters, and she had proof surely of that, there must also be witches and good fairies and spells and magic beasts? Perhaps there was some truth in all good stories, whether magic or not? What more was still lurking from the past even in the latter half of the twentieth century, even in the midst of television and supersonic aircraft and men landed by the most detailed of exact scientific instrumentation upon the moon? Did these things then not alter the basic magic of magic? So there always had been enchanters and always would be enchanters – and enchanted? And – how *old* was Mr Strange?

At about six o'clock the clouds began to lighten and a weak lemon-yellow sunlight tempted them out into the dripping meadow. Mrs Hearst organized Andrew and Laura into fetching eggs and milk from the farm and so they set off on the path across the field, Laura carrying the milk churn. William the cat appeared from nowhere and ran ahead of them, his tail held high. The wet grass smelled sweet and cold. After they had been served with the milk and eggs by fat, talkative Mrs Bryant, the farmer's wife, Laura and a pigtailed Ann who had appeared from an outside shed struck up a conversation, after a few minutes of staring and grinning at one another.

'How are you getting on down there?' asked Ann. 'Enjoying your holiday?'

'Yes, all right,' said Laura automatically.

'Where have you come from, then? London?'

'Yes.'

They began to talk about their respective schools and found that they were much the same age and the same year. Andrew turned, and bearing the eggs began to walk slowly back, while the two girls followed him, talking hard.

'What's the matter with him then?' asked Ann suddenly.

'Who?' Laura was taken aback for a moment.

'Why, your brother! Is he daft or what? His eyes are all swimmy-like, he doesn't look at one properly and – look! He's dropping the eggs!'

Andrew walking slowly straight ahead with the carton of eggs in his hands had stumbled over a large stone.

'Lucky there's none broke,' said Ann, helping to pick them up. 'But why is he so daft?'

'I don't know,' said Laura slowly. Andrew got up again without looking at them and went on, leaving Ann to carrry the eggs for him. 'At least, I *do* know,' said Laura swiftly, coming to a decision. She would try and tell Ann something: it would be such a relief.

'It's that odd old man who lives in one half of our house. He's done something to Andrew. He was quite all right before. He's hypnotized him. He's enchanted him.'

There, it was out. She had been able to tell someone, even if she would now be thought of as mad herself.

'Enchanted?' The word sounded odd in Ann's very broad accent. She giggled. 'I'll say he has,' she remarked. 'Look what he's doing now.'

Andrew had reached a stone wall. Instead of finding the stile which was not far away he clambered with difficulty to the top, balanced himself precariously and stood staring at the sun as it lit up the top of the hills far over the valley beyond them. There was one summit quite near, then behind it another, further and higher. It was this furthest ridge which his eyes were seeking. The yellow sunlight picked out a far line of steep-looking rocks and cliffs just beneath its highest point. It looked barren, formidable country. Behind it the clouds massed again, heavy and blue-black.

'You see,' said Laura, 'I don't know what to do. My parents won't notice. That Mr Strange: honestly, he does seem to have a kind of hold over Andrew.'

Ann seemed disposed to take quite a lively interest in Mr Strange.

'Mother and me were only saying this morning it was odd of Mrs Anderson letting him stay there like that,' she said. 'And we didn't seem to notice when he came. It must have only been a few days before you. Let me think. There were a lot of students the weekend before. We didn't get them all sorted out. But they were friends of Jimmy's, Mrs Anderson's son, you know. A strange, long-haired bunch. One had a guitar – no, not a proper guitar, an Indian thing – a zita or a zither or something he said it was called. They played this and they were up all night one night, at least we heard this zither-thing and all the lights were on. Mother now says she saw this old man about shortly after they all went. But she didn't think too much of it. Mrs Anderson has all sorts. Well, here's your eggs. I won't give them to him again.' They were outside Ramshead Lodge now. Laura glanced uneasily at the stable end of the house but the door was closed and there was no sign of Mr Strange.

'What shall I do about the enchantment?' she asked Ann casually, just as she was turning away, 'Have you any ideas how to break it?'

Ann laughed, tossing back her fat plait of hair. 'Search me,' she said. 'You'd better look in the fairy books, hadn't you? What do they do there? Answer riddles or something? What's that one called – Rumpelstiltskin? I was reading it to my little brother only last week. The girl there had to find out his name, don't you remember?'

'Yes, but I know Mr Strange's name,' said Laura doubtfully. Nevertheless her mind began to work, to remember.

There was that other story: *The Hobbit* – Bilbo and Gollum – they had asked each other riddles and Bilbo had Gollum's magic ring. They were deep down, far into the bowels of the earth, beneath a mountain.

'Well cheerio, I must be getting back to my tea; Mother was just putting the bacon on,' said Ann cheerfully. 'Will you be up tomorrow for anything? We could go a walk or something.'

'Yes, all right. Thanks.'

Laura watched her go, and felt a good deal better. She didn't believe that Ann had taken in the full gravity of the situation concerning Andrew, but then how could she so soon? She surely thought it some sort of make-believe game? Nevertheless she had put some ideas into Laura's head, and any idea was better than nothing; any help, any feeling that someone else was with her made a big difference. And Ann had obviously accepted Laura herself as a possible companion; she had accepted that Andrew was queer and daft, for whatever reason. It gave Laura an added relief too that Ann had noticed this strangeness of Andrew's right away for herself. There was no possible doubt: it wasn't all just in her own crazy imagination, as it had occurred to her uneasily that it might be. No: Andrew had altered. Andrew *was* under some sinister spell and now someone else knew of it.

He was still standing on the wall looking back at the hills. He was standing there when Laura went inside the house. He was there half an hour later, but when his mother went out to call him in to supper he dropped down as instantly and obediently as if he had just been clambering about the wall for fun.

'What's for supper then?' he asked as he picked himself up.

There can be no more normal and healthy sounding a question in a mother's ears than that, thought Laura in despair.

# six

Laura finally decided she was completely awake. She had been half awake and decidedly uncomfortable for some time. She was too hot, she was thirsty, she had had dreams which seemed to buzz round and round in her head like bees. There was something wound up like a gramophone record inside her which kept on repeating the words 'Dirty creatures, dirty creatures' until she was weary. Animals, birds, fish all came into her dreams and writhed and flapped and spoke.

First she sat up and tossed off half her bedclothes. Then she decided there was nothing else for it but a trip to the bathroom. The bedroom was impenetrably black. She could hear Andrew snoring slightly and regularly not far away on one side of her, so the door must be on the other. Resolutely she launched herself into the blackness, fumbling for the wall, the door, a light switch, anything to find out where she was. After what seemed a long walk but was in fact only a few hesitant paces, her hands encountered wall where she had expected to find the door. She felt totally muddled and disorientated then; wished to return but was not sure where her bed lay. At last, after another long, exposed time of reaching and stumbling and wishing herself back in the security of home where every movement necessary to midnight visits to the bathroom was a well-trodden and known track so that she had no need of light to accomplish it, she hit her forehead on the slightly open door and was out in the passage. She could still find no light switch but a little light came dimly up from the well of the stairs. The house breathed and creaked around her. There was a movement upon the stairs, small and continuous, and a chirruping cry. Something else stirred, was awake in no-man's-land; this stranger's house of sleep and dreams: the cat William had obviously been shut in by mistake and was asking to be let out.

He had reassured her rather than startled her. Something else existed and thought and wanted to be where it was not.

'All right, William,' she whispered. 'I'll let you out. Do you want to go hunting? Do you want to find lots of lovely mice?'

She slid back the bolt on the front door and opened it. William rubbed himself against her, he was a polite cat, and then suddenly rushed out. A breath of cool, earth-scented air came in with his exit; it had stopped raining but there was a gusty wind and a swishing and rushing of branches and grass. William vanished in an instant, swallowed into the blackness, bent upon his imperturbably, self-sufficient cat life. How simple it is, when you are a cat, thought Laura enviously.

By the time she returned to her room and found Andrew still sleeping, her bed just as she had left it, she felt she had been away half the night. Now she was able to sink into sleep as into a deep sea.

After a long period of dreamless unconsciousness she awoke suddenly to find it was dawn. Andrew lay on his back, arms stretched out, mouth open. Without any clear thought in her mind, she found herself up, and dressing. There was a thick ground mist and she could see the tops of trees more clearly than their trunks which were drowned in milky whiteness. Again, she was creeping up through a house that slept, though now the sleep was quieter, of a different kind and her restive brain had stilled. Again she slid the bolt back and opened the front door, this time to a faint shrilling of bird song. The sky was pink one side, pale, pale blue the other.

It was soaking wet in the grass outside the house, so she returned for her boots. Then she set off across the quiet meadow. A bird flew chittering before her. She climbed a stile and followed a path which led down to water-meadows at one side of the lake, along the lake and then up a valley on the far side. All about the water-meadows were the recumbent bodies of cows; some chewing with great breathy chumps and sighs, some motionless, wrapped in mist so she could hardly see them. Their eyes followed her movement, as she walked on, her mind feeling as half clear and half misty as the morning. Deep within the mist she sensed there were other creatures looking at her: she was near the borders of magic, yet whenever she stared full at a face or a figure that appeared at the corner of her eyes, it disappeared.

Sheep began to mingle with cows; the path wound upwards beside a stream and then it became more thickly wooded, the path steeper, and there was the growing sound of a waterfall. The stream was now in a narrow valley with wooded slopes on either side and just room for itself and the path which led round stones and boulders.

Then, after one particularly steep corner, Laura came upon a wide, secret little valley with a luxuriant grassy meadow on both sides of the stream, a waterfall at one end, and on the banks of the pool it made, a broken-down cottage. The cottage had a long time ago obviously been lived in, there was a chimney and windows and a door, but for many years it must have been used just as a shelter for sheep.

Laura walked right up to it. The sunlight strengthened, the mist was clearing rapidly. And whatever had been cloudy in her head cleared too, as suddenly as an entirely blocked-up deafened ear can clear, and just as one then seems to hear more distinctly than ever before, Laura could now see more distinctly than ever before, and she saw not the ruined, fallen stone, the sheep droppings she had expected to see, but a woman sitting inside looking at her. There was an odd feeling about the walls behind this woman, as if she was sitting in mist and water and moving light, but her face was ordinary enough. She was fiftyish, had brown hair with streaks of grey in it drawn back into a bun, a tanned, capable face, a slim and upright figure. She looked out at Laura and said pleasantly, though in a rather surprised voice:

'Why, I do believe you can see me.'

'Yes, I can,' replied Laura, and it was as if she had expected to meet this woman and she now knew why she had got up and made this long early morning walk. She could see her and realized about her that same half-enchantment she had felt at the beginning of it all by the lake, and again she became aware of strange animals moving higher on the moors above the tree line and of a presence, a silent watcher, among the highest stones on the top cliffs. But the faces had gone as the last of the mist vanished, dried out by the heat of the rising sun.

'You have been with strange company,' the woman said, looking questioningly at Laura. 'You have been in the company of an enchanter or you would never have seen me. You would have passed by an empty ruined cottage as everybody else does. You see, I'm not *in* this world, *in* time in the same way as you are. Wait a moment, come no nearer, I'll come out to you. This house is no fit place for you, sensitive as you are to it. You could get swept away. Come and sit on these smooth stones by the water and tell me how it is you have had to come looking for me.'

'But I didn't exactly know I was looking for you,' said Laura, obediently following the woman to the stones she had described. She was such a homely-looking, ordinary woman, Laura had no fear or shyness of her although she knew that she was a very magic person indeed; in some sense more different from herself and even more magic than Mr Strange.

'Didn't you?' said the woman comfortably.

There was a silence but for the noise of the water.

'Yes, I did,' said Laura. 'I felt you could help us. You see I'm all right, I know I'm all right really, but it's my brother Andrew,' and she found herself telling the whole story.

'Yes, of course,' said the woman, placidly and very prosaically, throwing a little stone into the water beside her. 'It's *that* one. He's up to his tricks again. Someone must have summoned him back, and of course he was only too delighted to have the opportunity for further mischief. But how foolish of whoever it was that brought him back!'

'How do you mean, brought Mr Strange *back*?' asked Laura in bewilderment.

'It's these silly people who will meddle with things they don't understand and call it "spiritualism": they summon up more than they know,' continued the woman thoughtfully. 'But there always are people somewhere who lay themselves open to forces of mischief and evil, and there always will be, I suppose.'

'I don't understand,' said Laura.

'The mischievous and cold-blooded enchanter you call "Mr Strange" lived and died in the body many years ago. He was a mortal who so corrupted and stretched himself by the practice of black arts that he became less mortal and so, after his natural death – and he managed to postpone that for many years – he could gain an entry back into this world if properly summoned. And that has happened, not once, but several times. He is so clever he can adapt himself easily to the manner and speech of whatever time he visits. And here he is again. Someone, or more probably some group of people, must have had a meeting, a séance or whatever they call it, quite recently and provided the bridge for him to return. They might not know at all what their experimenting had aroused. He might not have appeared directly to them.'

'You mean . . . I know!' cried Laura, a light dawning. 'It must have been those students staying in our house! Ann said they were an odd lot and stayed up all night and there were funny lights and noises! And then shortly after that Mr Strange was seen! But how could they bring him back like that? Is he a kind of ghost?'

'Ghost is one word people use for a spirit who will not rest,' said the woman. 'And I know that if your brother is showing all the symptoms of full enchantment, he is in real trouble and like to lose his body, and his soul as well, which is a far worse thing.'

'What can I do then?' cried Laura eagerly. 'Can you help me to undo the enchantment?'

'I wish I could, just like that, my dear. I cannot enter into his twisted mind. I can't undo the spells he has made. I can only advise you, and the first step you must take is to find out what questions he wants answered: enchanters are like trick boxes: work the right catch and they slide open and reveal what's inside. But the answers you must find for yourself.'

'You mean it *is* like Rumpelstiltskin, and *The Hobbit* and all the other stories,' said Laura slowly. 'But I'm hopeless at questions and riddles and impossible tasks. I shall never do it!' And tears began to drip down her nose. If she were not to be helped by magic how could she ever combat magic? It simply wasn't fair. She was only an ordinary girl and again she felt a great wave of frustration and impotence come up to overwhelm her. She began to tear at the pieces of rock and stone beside her, they crumbled remarkably easily and she threw the splinters of stone before her into the stream.

'Easy, my dear,' said the woman beside her. 'You have come a long way already in finding me and being able to talk to me. I'm not for common eyes, as I told you before. And you may find the questions not so difficult as you fear. You have a helper, a solid person of commonsense not far away. Whether she believes you literally or not does not matter. I see her now. Listen to her and don't dismiss her. Careful with the rock, you silly. Don't you see you're disturbing fossils and the husks of little sea creatures that have lain in that rock for thousands and millions of years?'

'Am I?' asked Laura, her tears dripping less swiftly. She looked at the stone she was holding and saw within it the fossilized remains of several shells and what looked like a petrified wood louse.

'Oh yes,' she said listlessly. 'We had a lesson on the fossils you find in some kinds of rock, once. You mean it was all sea here, once upon a time?'

'Yes, we're sitting on the beach in fact,' said the woman. 'And that very fossil you're holding now was alive even before my time: before any of us, before the watchers, the good or the evil ones. Before there was anything. You have seen more than most human beings ever dimly imagine. You have seen some of us and know, however slightly, how this world contains more than it seems. Now I shall show you its beginnings: not before life but before life became aware. We call them the Blind Times. You may not altogether like it, so hold my hand and stand up.'

The hand she reached to Laura's was warm and comforting, and it was just as well for as she stood slowly upright everything about her changed, her head swam, and she would have lost her balance.

She was standing upon a beach of coarse shingle and rock. Ahead of her was the sea: the unchanging sea that stays the same whatever the time in history, whatever the date of the world. It was a grey sea because the clouds were thick and low, although it was close and warm and somewhere not far behind the clouds was a faint yellow sun. There were low cliffs and rocks to one side of her, on the other a sluggish stream lost itself in livid patches of marsh and pools of scummy water upon which unnamed slimy things crawled. There were further slimy, writhing things coming in and out, in and out with the little waves that broke with a gently shushing noise upon the beach. Behind her, stretching for several miles was a strip of lowish land covered with grasses and ferns and low, palm-like trees rather like pine-apples. Behind this was a range of mountains marching away into the distance, several with cone-like peaks, some erupting, others black and silent. There was no noise, except for the slap of the sea and a constant distant rumble from the volcanoes. A flickering glow lit up the sky over the mountain ranges, but the colours were dim; this was no bright morning of the world, dazzling in its clarity; it was cloudy and hazy, the light was muted, the colours dull red, yellowish-grey and green.

There was nothing else. There were no great trees or plants or flowers. It was before the time of the coal forests. It was before any time she had ever heard about or seen created by a museum or the illustration to a book on pre-history. Nothing else, no movement that came from any living thing except an insignificant sea creature for miles and miles, for thousands of miles, for ever. For the whole world. There was a thin smell of sulphur and of course vegetation and of the sea, but no more. No reek of mammal bodies, no reptiles, no sea birds, nothing. Nothing with anything like nostrils to smell, nothing with anything like eyes to see, nothing with anything like ears to hear.

The loneliness, the apartness, the intolerable feeling of waiting – for what? – for nothing, because nothing of any significance to man could happen here for millions upon millions of years, became so oppressive to Laura, so alien from anything she had ever experienced in her life, that she screamed: 'Oh! I'm suffocating, take me back, take me back!'

She still somehow had hold of a warm, comforting hand. The sound of the sea turned into that of the waterfall and a hundred other homely sounds: the chatter of birds, the plop of a rising fish, a breath of wind in the trees, a far-off dog barking and an even farther-off human voice calling to someone.

'See how much better this is,' said the woman, still holding her hand. 'Even though you've fallen into deep trouble? See how busy the world is, even here, far from the cities? You are not alone and can never be alone as aloneness really is. No man or woman in this world now, far out in a little boat on the ocean, deep in a cave, high on a mountain top or shut in a prison cell can be one thousandth as alone as you for a few seconds were. And that is because of the growing of life and of those both good and evil who assemble to watch over life growing.'

Laura knew there were a great many questions she wanted to ask. But instead she found herself yawning and yawning, she was so tired and sleepy she could scarcely stand upright.

'Who are you?' she managed to say between one immense yawn and another.

The woman laughed. 'Well, I suppose in every enchantment there is a good fairy of some kind, and that is the nearest I can get to it for you. You don't see me as I really am, of course. Yes, the old stories may have been muddled and mistaken in places, but the bones of them were true enough. So there really were and still are enchantments and witches and fairies and passing of souls from one body into another and people who attain a near immortality who live on and off about the ordinary world. I suppose it's not unlike taking a walk in a garden, cutting off the dead heads, plucking a flower here or there: only some of us care about it for the growing plant's sake and others care for nothing but their own amusement . . . You must go back now, I am becoming too much for you. Turn round straight away and good luck go with you.'

Without a word of farewell Laura stumbled away over the stones. At the stone wall she looked back. The cottage stood empty. The woman was gone. The sound of the water went on and on in her ears, confusing her yet further. It took a long time to die away.

When she reached Ramshead Lodge the curtains were still drawn. She let herself quietly in at the front door. The sitting room clock said five to eight. There was the sound of running water from the bathroom as if one of her parents were getting up. She went into her bedroom to find Andrew still asleep in the position she had left him.

'Mr Strange is a ghost,' she said quietly, testing herself. She felt so sleepy the words meant nothing. He had come back from the dead; he had lived many, many years ago. Five seconds later Laura was stretched upon her bed, as deeply asleep as her brother.

## seven

'Upon my word, Laura, you're not very good-tempered today,' said Mrs Hearst at breakfast. 'You needn't bite my head off. I only wanted to know if you wanted some more coffee. And try not to yawn so noisily, darling. Andrew, *do* mind where you're putting the marmalade! You just don't look, do you? Honestly children, I do wish you could behave in a more civilized fashion at meal times.'

Laura paid little attention to her mother's words. They were very normal. Her father was reading the newspaper a little apart from the breakfast table as if he did not wish to be associated too closely with his family and that was very normal too. But looking at Andrew and what he was *now* doing to the marmalade made a little thrill of fear run through her and brought her to full consciousness. She had only been half awake before. Because Andrew had changed yet again. At the beginning of his enchantment he had been aloof, abstracted: there had been within him an unpleasant vein of controlled distaste for her: she had felt that when he deigned to notice her he disliked her because in some way she stood between him and whatever he desired. Now Laura sensed his hostility was slackening and though this was a relief to her, in a sense she was uneasier than ever, because whatever control he had over himself was slackening too. It was the fifth day of his enchantment. He looked flushed, excited. He took a mouthful of food, then forgot to eat and sat with his mouth slightly open, staring ahead. Then, with a start, as if recalled to what he was doing he would chew for a moment, pause, and sit vacant again. The marmalade he chased absent-mindedly about the table with his knife, then appeared to forget it altogether.

Mrs Hearst reprimanded him for this rude stretching over the table and chasing of the marmalade pot, but then returned to a letter she was reading.

'Mummy, *do* look at Andrew,' tried Laura, filled with a sudden surge of irritation and desire to shake her mother into noticing his condition.

A day ago Andrew would have replied with composure: he would have said 'What is there to look at?' or something similar, and behaved, while his mother's eye was upon him, with absolute normality. Now he hardly seemed to hear what Laura said and continued vaguely to butter his plate instead of the piece of toast which had fallen unseen upon the table-cloth.

Laura had a moment of hope. 'Look!' she cried urgently.

'What is it now?' Her mother looked up vaguely for a moment then her eyes returned immediately to her letter.

'Such a long letter from Mrs Anderson in Florence,' she remarked. 'She seems very anxious that we should be having a good time. I think she must be a nice woman. But she doesn't put an exact address on her letter, bother her. Oh well. I don't really especially want to write to her at this stage. There's a lot of interesting stuff about this house, children. The history of it. You can read the letter afterwards if you like.'

'Mummy!' cried poor Laura.

'Oh, do stop *shouting* at me, Laura. Really I don't know what's the matter with you today,' exclaimed her mother in an irritated voice, getting up and beginning to clear the table.

'Have you finished, Andrew? What a mess you seem to have made of your plate. Hand it up, there's a good boy.'

'Mummy, Andrew was putting butter all over his plate,' tried Laura once more, but as she said it she knew it was hopeless. The words came out in a kind of disagreeable whine, and were not attended to, although the whine was.

'Don't talk to your mother like that,' said her father, suddenly and briskly coming to life from behind his paper.

Andrew meanwhile said nothing but carried the pot of marmalade into the kitchen, stumbling over a mat as he did so. He put the pot on the draining-board and turned. His eyes were fixed ahead of him, rather upwards, and were full; full of his vision; they appeared to Laura to give off a positive ray of light; he stumbled out, his eyes fixed so far away he hardly seemed to see the objects near at hand, but he at least went through the motions of clearing the table and his parents noticed nothing, nothing.

To be not adult and not taken seriously can be one of the worst things in the world. Laura could stand it no longer.

'Oh, I *hate* you *all*!' she cried out bitterly and fled upstairs to the sanctuary of her bedroom. For the moment she had completely given up.

But there is a limit to the amount of time one can spend sobbing upon one's bed, feeling utterly misjudged and misunderstood. Before so very long Laura's natural resilience and the good spirits which she normally possessed, which are so often a matter of luck rather than natural goodness because they are based upon an excellent health and constitution, began to assert themselves. She realized too that not only the pillow into which she had been crying was damp but so still was the lower part of her skirt where it had been soaked by the long wet grass. Yes, it had happened. It had not all been some kind of queer dream. She had gone out and encountered a – a someone – and she was the better for it. She had not given up; the growing fear of she knew not quite what was still there but she could not counter it. She would tackle Mr Strange: she felt no fear of him, indeed she was almost coming to like him, he was so polite and mild. There was something companionable and easy about him. She was eager to talk further with him, to learn more. Ghost or no, he did not frighten her, he was too real; too much of this day and age.

Unaware that there was danger in this swing of mood, this attraction to her enemy, the cleverness of whose art she had so dim a comprehension, Laura brushed her hair, humming as she did so, and ran briskly downstairs.

They were all in the sitting room, now swept and cleared of all traces of breakfast. Andrew sat upon the corner of the table, winding and unwinding a ball of string. Mr and Mrs Hearst had a map spread out upon the table and were studying paths and contour lines. 'The Pennine Way is only a stone's throw from this house,' Laura heard. 'It combines with the Roman Road, here, and runs right up and over Great Shunner Fell – look – one could walk it just as far as one felt like: perhaps you could meet me at Thwaite.'

Upon the table lay Mrs Anderson's letter which Laura glanced at casually as she passed. She caught the words:

'. . . Isabella Strangeway who built the house for herself and her son after her was apparently a great eccentric . . . There is a story that she made London too hot to hold her, and that her son was as bad and that this was partly why they came so far up here to . . .' Mrs Anderson's writing was so bad it became an increasing effort to read any further. Anyway Laura's mind was on other things.

She opened the front door and stepped outside into the sunshine. If she had any hopes of evading Andrew and visiting Mr Strange on her own they were quickly dashed, for the moment she began to saunter casually along the path to the stables he was out too, and following her.

'Good morning, Laura, good morning, Andrew,' said Mr Strange's voice pleasantly as he emerged from the lower part of the stables which was kept for gardening tools and logs. 'What a fresh day it is too, after the rain yesterday.'

Laura hurried up to him.

'You have to make me answer questions,' she said. 'If I can do them you finish the enchantment, that's right isn't it?'

'Oh, so all memory of the proper procedure has *not* quite died out,' remarked Mr Strange, looking for a moment a little put out. 'But no matter, you won't find the questions easy, you know. There are two questions, as a matter of fact, and one, well I suppose one could call it one event which must be brought about. You see how good I am at modern idiom? I believe there's such a word too as "non-event" and that, my dear Laura, will be all the result of your labours because however clever you may be at questions, the last task will tax you beyond your powers, indeed it will. Andrew, my dear, come and sit by me and let me have a good look at you.'

'I'm ready for the first question,' said Laura stoutly, facing Mr Strange, her fists unconsciously clenching and unclenching themselves.

'Oh, very well,' he said with a rather petulant sigh, dropping a little magnifying glass hanging on a chain round his neck through which he had been peering attentively at Andrew's eyes.

'You are within your rights, of course. Well, the first question I must ask you is—

'Where are the souls I have already enchanted and what bodily form do they take?'

The question rang senselessly in Laura's ears. For a few seconds she could make nothing of it: *what bodily form do they take?* Whatever did he mean by that? He had enchanted others before Andrew: well, that was likely enough, so what had happened to them? To their own bodies? Their bodies were finished. Laura jibbed at the word 'died', but something of the sort must have happened, and so, and so, their souls were – where *were* their souls? – how could this be?

She was aware of a great and growing silence and her fear came up into her throat and her heart pounded and her ears roared. Mr Strange looked at her steadily and a little smile on his lips grew and grew.

'You don't think that bodily death makes me relinquish my hold,' he said gently. 'Why, half the fun is keeping them afterwards, you know. I must put them somewhere.'

And then Laura became aware of what she could only describe as a tickle in her brain. It was as if she were a clock and Mr Strange, with his delicate, womanish fingers (the nails were longish, like a woman's, the fingers tapering) were tinkering gently among her inner mechanisms. And somewhere in there she had a picture of the lake, down to which they had gone at the very beginning of all the magic, and within the lake she saw huge fish moving, and they had mouths and lips and faces.

'The fish in the lake,' she almost cried out. 'You mean the souls of the enchanted are in the fish.' She remembered the fairy story she had read; she remembered other stories. It seemed so likely to be in the fish. But then she paused, in the very act of opening her mouth. For she realized that she was being manipulated: that Mr Strange wanted her to answer with the word 'fish' and she would be wrong: he was misleading her. She had not thought about the fish being aware since she had half succumbed to the enchantment herself: they had taken no part in her later vision of some benevolent presence near a waterfall of creatures moving high on the moors above, of a watcher in the highest stones.

*Where* had Andrew seen Mr Strange walking, and *what* had he been holding? It was there that Andrew had first been attracted to him, had said that he wanted to talk to him, and she had idly wondered why. Up on those moors there were beasts whose strangeness she was only just beginning to comprehend . . .

'Wait!' cried Laura desperately as she saw Mr Strange begin to shake his head and say: 'I hate to remind you, but there is a time limit; we have to set a time limit, you know.'

'Wait! They are up on the moors – what are they called?' the name Great Shunner Fell came into her mind and was rejected. No, that was miles off, upon the Pennine Way. The moors in question were – she had it – her father had named all the hills about while they were picnicking.

'They are up on the moors which are called Firedale Forest, where Ramshead Gill rises, below High Scar Edge and Stony Head Pike and they are sheep!' she cried. Mr Strange had come down from the moors holding a shepherd's crook, the day they had been pony trekking, and now she knew what he had been doing. He had been counting his flock.

'The souls you have enchanted are in the sheep that feed

up on the moors under High Scar Edge,' she said again clearly and steadily, and she knew without a shadow of doubt that she was right, even before she saw his face change.

# eight

The momentary expression of annoyance left Mr Strange's face very rapidly, however, and within seconds it was as smooth and bland as it had ever been.

'The first question has been answered correctly,' he said in measured tones. 'And now for the second. You may or may not be aware that Mr Strange is not my real name. Now I must ask you what my full name is: my baptismal name. At least . . .' He paused and added an afterthought in a lighter tone of voice, 'not that I actually *was* baptized, now the subject arises. It was considered very odd in those days not to be, I assure you. As for *when* it was that I was named it is not part of your business to have to answer, but I can tell you that I am older than I look, by a long way. I flatter myself that I am most excellently preserved.'

'Your real name,' echoed Laura thoughtfully. She was still elated at answering the first question correctly and did not this time experience any feeling of despair. Instead she felt strongly that this question lay within her power to answer: it did not need any inspired guesswork or the aid of any lingering vestige of semi-enchantment.

For why had Mr Strange come back from whatever shadowy land of the dead or half-dead he had inhabited to this particular house? Why did he describe the room above the stables as his little home? Was it not because the house had indeed once been his? *What* was the rhyme above the door and *what* was it Mrs Anderson had written to her mother?

'The woman who built the house was called Isabella—' and the name had looked oddly half familiar to her eyes on the writing paper, although her mind had been so preoccupied at the time. Isabella, who had been a great eccentric. Didn't that mean very odd, perhaps a little mad? Perhaps a little *magic*?

Laura buried her face in her hands. She was sure she was somehow on the right track, but this time she had none of the facts at her fingertips. He would want an exact, precise answer, the full name. If she answered vaguely and only half correctly she would get no second chance.

Mr Strange began to hum a little tune. 'Perhaps it is my duty to tell you the time limit,' he said gaily. 'For the first question which by some lucky guess you managed to answer within ten minutes, you had in fact half an hour. For the second question you have one hour. For the third—'

'Oh, don't let's bother about the third now!' cried Laura desperately. An idea came to her.

'I don't have to answer it standing here, do I? I can go back to my room and think there?'

'Yes, I suppose that is within the rules,' replied Mr Strange after a moment's hesitation. 'But you must return here precisely at, let me see—' He consulted a gold watch which he had drawn out of his trouser pocket— 'at twelve o'clock.'

For once Laura abandoned Andrew, who continued sitting at the bottom of the stable steps. Mr Strange mounted them and withdrew into his room while Laura ran into the main part of the house, pausing a moment on the threshold to read again:

Num mea
Mox huius
Sed postea
Nescio quius

Where was her mother? Where was her mother's letter?

'Mummy! Mummy!' she cried, running wildly about the house. She finally ran her to earth in the pantry.

'Mummy, please, quickly, where's that letter about the history of this house from Mrs Anderson? I want to read it.'

'Why now all of a sudden? You didn't take much interest earlier on, you funny girl. Look, isn't it annoying, all this milk has gone sour, I wonder if there is thunder in the air? There's nothing to beat milk in bottles and a proper fridge really, you know.'

'Yes, yes,' said Laura, in agony, 'the letter, please, where is it? Oh, I do so want to read it!'

'Well now, since you're so keen, and you'll find it very interesting too, what did I do with it? I know I didn't tear it up or throw it away. It might be in my handbag. Or up on my dressing-table. Or, wait, it just might be—'

But Laura had gone.

It took a quarter of an hour to track the letter down; Laura finally discovered it in a book her mother had been reading and bore it in haste to her room. Ten minutes later she was downstairs again, trying to control her frustration and knowledge that time was inexorably ticking on and on. She must not spoil things now by shrieking at her mother desperately: she must control herself and ask politely. It was a very great effort.

She came up to her mother in the kitchen.

'Please do you mind, but could you read it to me?' she begged. 'I've been trying and trying and I can make out some of the words, but Mrs Anderson has such very difficult handwriting and I don't want to miss anything.'

'Hasn't she just!' agreed her mother rather absent-mindedly. 'I will read the letter with pleasure, darling, but just let me finish these three scones while I've got flour all over my hands. I was more or less forced to make them, you see, because of all that sour milk. That reminds me, we'll need some extra milk down from the farm some time.'

'I'll get it later,' promised Laura, in agony. Over half the time had gone now. She ran back to check with the clock in the sitting room. It was nearly twenty to twelve. How long did it take to make scones, for heaven's sake?

After seven long minutes they were finally in the oven. Mrs Hearst's hands were clean and she took up the letter, smiling at Laura's interest.

She began to read, then paused. 'It's not all here. It goes from page 2 to page 5. There's a page 3 and 4 somewhere about. You must have dropped it.'

'Oh goodness,' exclaimed Laura weakly. She saw it all now. This was some trick of his; she was so near and yet so far; he was laughing at her, and she would never find pages 3 and 4, which of course might be the very ones to give his names. She could never have had pages 3 and 4 in her bedroom, which had added to her difficulty in reading the letter and making sense of it. If only she had not been in such a flap. If only she could calm down. She stood, clenching and unclenching her fists, trying to master herself. There were still twelve minutes left.

Meanwhile her mother had gone briskly out of the room.

'Here it is, you careless thing,' she said, returning a minute later. 'Dropped upon the stairs. Just let me get it into order. Here we are.

' "Dear Mrs Hearst . . ." '

At five minutes to twelve Laura pushed aside the motionless Andrew, still sitting like a devoted little dog outside the door of the man who owned him. She ran up the steps and knocked at the closed door.

'If you are asking for more time, I cannot give it, you know,' he said expectantly, opening the door and bringing out his watch.

'I don't want any more time,' cried Laura, blessing again and again the loquacious, letter-writing Mrs Anderson, all seven pages of her. 'I've found out who you are, or were. I've found out a lot about you. Your name is Robert Edward Strangeway, son of Isabella Strangeway. I don't know when you were born exactly and that doesn't matter, but it must have been before 1667, before the house was built. "Now mine, soon his, but afterwards I don't know whose." Well, the house is Mrs Anderson's now and she's been looking up all sorts of old books and deeds, because she's interested in that sort of thing, and she found out the names of several of the other owners. This house was an inn once, too. And there were stories about the goings on there! Mrs Anderson has written it all in her letter to Mummy. She wrote that when you lived in the house after your mother's death, the people in the farmhouses and cottages round about told odd stories about your visitors and said that you had supped with the Devil himself!'

'Never, he doesn't exist, and if he did exist I would never have lowered myself to have supper with someone so low-born and degenerate,' snapped Mr Strange, visibly taken off balance. 'The disagreeable things people will say! Oh, all right, you have got it somehow: I didn't realize I was so well known. It's flattering really. Yes, my full name is Robert Edward Strangeway, you have guessed my second question correctly. You can call me Mr Strangeway or Mr Strange or Robert for all I care. But don't get cocky, my girl, for the third thing you will never do.'

'And what is that?' cried Laura, flushed and emboldened by her success. 'You just ask me and see.'

Mr Strange – she still thought of him as Mr Strange and indeed it was a suitable enough name – Mr Strange folded his arms, looked straight ahead and declaimed in a singsong voice:

'You have answered my first two questions correctly and this has never been done before: you are cleverer than I thought, but I have my victim nearly fast now and I will not loosen my hold until the time when a great singing beast and a pair of talking wings come together and rebuke me.'

A great singing beast and a pair of talking wings. Oh, the unfairness of it! For this must be pure magic and to this Laura could have no answer. How could she conjure up a magic beast from the hills: was she to roam about there, trying to find one? How could she cope?

'I thought that would prove a little difficult,' said Mr Strange, looking down at her complacently. 'And for this third task you have until the end.'

'Until the end?' asked Laura. 'What do you mean?'

A little smile hovered about his lips. 'I mean until the natural end: the end of the enchantment,' he said gently, almost considerately. 'We should not have so very long to wait now. Good morning to you.'

And he clapped shut his door and disappeared inside. Then two things happened. Andrew got up from where he had been sitting at the bottom of the steps and began to stumble blindly across the meadow, walking directly through a clump of nettles without so much as looking down at them, and at that moment a little red sports car turned in at the gate and drove down towards the house. Slowly as it was going Andrew somehow contrived not to see it; his path lay across it; there was a bump, a screech of brakes and Andrew stumbled and fell, as far as Laura could judge, directly under the car's wheels.

'Andrew!' she cried desperately into the sudden shocked silence.

## nine

'I simply can't imagine how you could have been so silly or what you thought you were doing, Andrew!' exclaimed Mrs Hearst for the fifth or sixth time. They were all inside the house now: Andrew shaken but apparently unhurt, a strange young man and a girl, Laura and her father.

'I couldn't have been looking where I was going,' said Andrew for the third or fourth time. Laura saw with relief that his fall seemed to have temporarily at any rate shocked some kind of sense into him.

'Well, we're awfully sorry it happened at all,' said the young man for the second time. He was a redhead with a red curly beard, and curly red hair on his chest which showed through his green shirt. He wore glasses and though rather homely in appearance, looked a friendly and lively personality. The girl had long fair hair, sandy eyelashes and a pale, unmade-up face. They both wore tattered, rather dirty jeans and plimsolls.

'Mrs Anderson did tell you we might be coming?' said the young man. 'Just for the one night, you know. We're on our way back from Scotland.'

'No, we've heard nothing about you,' said Mrs Hearst blankly, looking round at her husband for support. 'For the *night*, you say?'

'Dear, oh dear, that sounds typical enough of Moira Anderson,' said the young man cheerfully. 'Well, don't let us put you out then, Mrs Hearst. We've sleeping-bags in the car. We can doss down in the stable or something. I'd better introduce us, too. I'm Ron. I'm an old friend of Jimmy Anderson's. And this is Cath. We were all up together the other weekend with Jimmy and some others. There was quite a party. Then Cath and I went up to Scotland to tour round a bit and Jimmy said he'd clear it with his mother to let us break our journey here on the way down again. He said he was sure you wouldn't mind. Cath can have the extra bedroom and I can squeeze in the parlour or on the floor of her room or anywhere. That's right, isn't it, Cath?'

'Yeah,' said Cath, blinking her sandy eyelashes amiably.

'But if you hadn't heard anything about it and don't fancy us, just give the word and we'll camp in the stables. We have sleeping-bags and we've got a little oil stove and we were taking an evening meal off some friends near here anyway—'

'Oh well, I should think you had better be in the house,' said Mrs Hearst slowly. 'I do wonder at Mrs Anderson and

Jimmy not – oh well. Now you're here, you're here. And in fact you might help us solve a little problem my husband and I were just discussing. Tell you what. Let's all have a cup of tea.'

'Yeah,' agreed Cath, almost with enthusiasm.

Round the teacups Mr and Mrs Hearst's problem was settled before Laura realized the full import of what was being arranged.

'You see my husband wants to walk over some miles of the Pennine Way; but it's a there-and-back walk unless I can drive to a meeting point and bring him home in the car,' explained Mrs Hearst. 'I was going to do this: perhaps drive to Thwaite or somewhere like that, but it would take time and I'd either have to drag the children with me or leave them for what might be some time on their own. But if you're going to be around this afternoon they can do as they please.'

'*I* don't want to drive round half the afternoon,' said Andrew swiftly.

'I didn't think you would, darling, but now if we get Daddy off right away with a packed lunch I can drive over about five o'clock or however long we reckon it will take and meet him. And you can muck about here: try Daddy's rod as he said you could or whatever you like. I shouldn't be away more than a couple of hours at most. When were you going to dinner, Ron?'

'Oh, not until sevenish. And we wouldn't be late back to disturb you. We'll be in by ten or so, won't we, Cath?'

'Yeah,' said Cath.

'That's fine then,' said Mr Hearst getting up briskly. 'I'll get ready to get off. See you this evening. If I'm flaked out after the walk and we want to go to bed early we'll leave the door unlatched.'

It was all arranged: suddenly it struck home to Laura that she would be alone, or more or less alone, with Andrew for two hours that afternoon, that her parents though outwardly useless and unnoticing about Andrew had yet been comforting to have about the place. She had a terrible sense of fore-boding.

'Do you have to go to meet him, Mummy?' she tried weakly when she got her mother alone for a moment in the kitchen. 'Why can't Daddy walk back again or stay the night somewhere or something?'

'Laura, don't be silly. This is much the best way of arranging it. And having these two around anyway most of the time makes me much easier in my mind. Even if the car breaks down or something we wouldn't be leaving you alone late at night. They seem quite a nice couple – but really – I don't know – one doesn't generally expect people renting one's country cottage to put up all and sundry. Mrs Anderson is really *too* casual. But perhaps this isn't her fault: it's Jimmy's. Out of my way, duck. I just want to put in something for Daddy to drink.'

It was useless. And Laura knew it would be hopeless to try and persuade Andrew to take the trip in the car. She would go herself, but then he would remain at the house on his own and that would be worse. She didn't think that Ron and Cath would be much use to her: how could they? They had not driven all this way to be nursemaids to a half-demented enchanted boy.

Time gathered pace and inevitability, like a river fed and swollen by increasingly swift flowing streams. Mr Hearst strode off in his stoutest shoes, rucksack on back. Laura, Andrew and Mrs Hearst had lunch. At least Laura and her mother had lunch. Andrew pushed his food around his plate but this drew no comment. Cath and Ron had a bottle of beer and bread and cheese outside by the car, for Ron had the bonnet open and appeared to be taking most of its insides out while Cath settled herself beside him with a sketch pad and began to draw the house. She was an art student, it appeared; a pleasant, but very silent girl, as if her fingers and pencil could do most of the talking for her.

It seemed no time at all after lunch before Mrs Hearst snapped her book shut and said brightly: 'Well, I think I'll be getting off now. It's not four yet but it'll take half an hour or so to get there and the light is so lovely that once I've parked the car I think I'll stroll up a bit of the way to meet him. There should be some gorgeous views over the top. But there's quite a wind: I wouldn't be surprised if it didn't rain later. Come and see me out of the drive, Laura, it's a brute of an exit and I don't want to scrape the car.'

Ron winked at Laura as she walked despondently back down the drive, after waving goodbye to her mother.

'Hey, what you going to do with yourself now Mum's away?' he said cheerfully. 'Why, I believe you've got company already.'

Laura turned to see Ann leaning over the gate. 'Like to come for a walk?' she called.

'I don't know. I don't know what Andrew wants to do.' And where was Andrew? She had left him inside, idly pushing together the pieces of a jigsaw puzzle; was he still there?

'Hello, Ann!' said Ron heartily, straightening up, pushing his hand down his open shirt and scratching the hairs on his chest with his oily fingers.

'Helloah,' replied Ann. She climbed the gate and walked down the drive. 'Oh, it's you two back again, is it? You're Jimmy's great friend, aren't you? You were with that bunch the other weekend.'

'Yeah.' Cath pushed her hair back from her forehead. 'Do you think it's like?' She held up her pencil sketch of the house.

'Oo, not *bad*,' said Ann. 'Is it, Laura?'

'It's jolly good,' said Laura, impressed. Cath didn't look capable of such a neat and detailed piece of work.

'You had a proper old party that weekend,' remarked Ann, who had obviously been bored and had visibly brightened at the sight of some company. 'We heard you at three o'clock in the morning still at it and that twanging zither-thing.'

'I'm sorry if we disturbed you,' Ron grinned. 'Yes, that was quite a night. It wasn't our fault was it, Cath? It was that greasy, middle-aged bloke and his zombie-like friend who seemed to be completely under his thumb. To tell you the truth I don't remember that night all that well. We were a bit tight, weren't we, Cath?'

'*I* wasn't,' returned Cath, just a little tartly.

'Laura here says you raised something,' continued Ann in a rather provocative voice. 'A funny-looking old fellow, who's now living in the loft, and he's put Andrew under some spell or other.'

'I didn't say that exactly,' protested Laura, in an agony of embarrassment. She needed help so much but she could not bear to be laughed at, and they would laugh at her; they would not take it seriously.

'That's odd.' Ron straightened up again and frowned.

'There was some sort of a silly carry-on,' he said. 'A five-sided figure chalked out and chants and invocations and I don't know what all. I wasn't feeling very interested in any of it by that time, to tell the truth.'

'Don't you remember that crash, Ron?' Cath now laid aside her work and seemed almost animated. 'There was a kind of rending crash and a cold wind, but nothing after that.'

'And someone made some silly joke and we all went to bed: at least we didn't all *have* a bed that weekend, did we? We turned in and dossed down somewhere or other.'

'I don't believe that fat bloke and his nasty friend did,' said Cath. 'They went on sitting cross-legged and looking perfect owls. They cleared off next day, do you remember? I didn't go for those two very much. I can't think why Jimmy asked them. They didn't fit in.'

'Tell us more about the old man,' suggested Ron.

'He's living up there,' said Ann, giggling and pointing. 'I've not seen him near to myself. But Laura has, haven't you, Laura?'

'Let's go and say hello,' suggested Ron. Cath too seemed interested. She had walked to the bottom of the stable steps.

'The top door's open,' she called, 'But I can't see anyone inside.'

'Do look out,' moaned Laura half to herself. She felt powerless to intervene. But in a moment Cath was descending the steps. 'There *might* have been someone in there,' she reported. 'But there isn't much sign of him now.'

Laura and Ann ran up behind her. Laura was too amazed to say anything. For the loft was – just a loft. A pile of straw and old sacks lay in one corner. The remains of one or two very yellowed newspapers strewed the floor. An old hayfork was propped up against a wall. There was no furniture: no sign of him whatsoever. There was not even a fireplace . . . She had to look again, but there was no fireplace. Indeed, on thinking of it, it would have been most unusual to have had a fireplace and chimney running through the stables to the loft above. But she had seen the logs burning. Seen the smoke!

'He was here: it's all different, it's all changed,' she said weakly.

'I suppose an old tramp could have been here,' said Ron. 'A funny coincidence isn't it, when they were trying to raise – who was it Cath, Beelzebub or one of those old codgers?'

'Don't ask me,' replied Cath. She made a face and shrugged her shoulders and they walked down the steps, laughing. Of course they believed nothing had happened: of course. It was too improbable. But though Ann had laughed too, she looked in a friendly way at Laura.

'Funny thing,' she was beginning doubtfully, when Laura suddenly saw Andrew.

He must have come out of the front door when her attention was diverted. Now he was two fields away, stumbling on the same path she had taken that had brought her to the waterfall the other morning. He was travelling quickly but every now and then he fell over or walked into a tree or displayed some other sign of not being in full control of his body. It was as if he were being irresistibly drawn on a certain track: as a piece of steel is drawn towards a magnet.

'Andrew!' called Laura, and then: 'Wait for me, I'm coming Andrew. I'm coming too!'

She clambered over the wall and set off in pursuit. She heard the others laughing at her prompt departure, but they made no move to follow her. She turned once, at the next wall, to catch a glimpse of Ann and Cath chatting together. Ron had returned to his car.

Then Laura ran after Andrew as fast as she could, mounting anxiety hastening her stride.

## ten

It was not long before Laura realized that Andrew was taking the same path she had found the other morning when she had gone out into the early morning mist. Though he was travelling quickly, he was walking rather than running and although he had a good start she was gradually, in spite of pounding heart and aching legs, able to close the gap between them. Luckily she was wearing plimsolls which were good for running. By the time they came to the little secret valley which had the waterfall at its head, she was nearly up with him. He was scrambling over a gap in the wall, paused to jump, and she had him by the legs.

'Andrew, where are you going? Do stop,' she had just the breath to gasp.

He turned and looked at her and she winced from the stare and glare of his eyes.

'Let me, leave me – I must get *on*,' he muttered incoherently.

'No!' She grappled with him, half on the wall, half not, and they fell together into a patch of bracken on the other side. Luckily neither of them was hurt.

Laura made full advantage of being the bigger and heavier, and as they got up made sure she had Andrew's arm twisted behind his back.

'Let me go!' he writhed but could not break away. He ran on a few steps with Laura still wrestling with him. 'Please,' she cried, 'Please Andrew, don't. Don't be like that!'

'You can't stop me. You mustn't. There's no stopping—'

With a desperate movement he kicked her shin. It would have hurt much more if he'd been in heavy shoes but like Laura he was wearing plimsolls. As it was she said 'Ouch!' and dropped her hold. He ran on, then when nearly at the ruined hut, swerved, turned, took a few paces back and Laura coming up behind him was able to grab him again. He shuddered once and stood still, his face twisted away from her and away from the woman who had turned him and made him run.

Laura had not seen her until that moment. Again she had the sensation of the light about her being disturbed, but this time the woman's body trembled with the waves of light that were passing through it; she was less real, less easy to see and there was a roaring in Laura's ears, both from the waterfall and from something within herself. Nevertheless she held firm.

'Please help us, you must please help us,' she cried. 'Here he is, this is my brother I was telling you about, and you can see what he is like. I did manage to answer two of the questions, but now I must find a singing beast with a pair of talking wings and this sounds pure magic and I can't be expected to do such a thing on my own! Does such a thing exist anyway? Oh I wish I understood!'

'I can help you a little, with the magic of chance,' the woman answered. 'But that is not the end of it. You have to stand firm. Remember that.'

'Oh, I don't understand,' cried Laura again. 'Are there magical beasts or aren't there? And I thought I saw faces, odd faces in the trees. Oh, I wish I knew what I saw! What was true and what wasn't?'

'Well, you saw me,' said the woman. 'I exist, though not in the same way as you, or for that matter in the same way as an enchanter such as your Mr Strange. You see, to work his magic at all he had to use real visions among the false. Do you understand that? Nothing you saw was *entirely* false, but he muddled Time, he opened your eyes beyond mortal limits, so that you saw what had been, and what could be, and probably also many elemental spirits that can never have bodies and exist in the same way that you exist.'

'Do you mean that there *were* once talking beasts?' began Laura.

'Not perhaps in the way you are thinking. But had you never thought that when men were more like animals, animals may have been more like men? Every mammal has a kinship even now, and once was closer to other species within that kinship. There was a time, for instance, when men and the great apes could understand each other a good deal better than they do today, before they grew apart from one another. You see, when conscious life began, it was like the flickering up of many candle flames: then after a time, one kind, the human kind, began to burn high and steadily, while the others settled down more into the stumps of the candles. Cows are more simply just cows; dogs more simply dogs than they once might have been. There was more room for experiment in the old days. This is where some of the talking beasts of the fairy tales come from; there is still the faint memory among men that some few animals did once have the power of some speech – just a few pioneers, as indeed it was just a few pioneers who have led mankind on to become so much more than the beasts.'

'Oh,' said Laura, her brain so full of new ideas it felt like bursting. 'And the – the *thing* that watches from the top up there somewhere: I feel it now, and it sends cold shivers down my spine!'

'You mean the Watcher at the top of Stony Pike? No normal person need fear him today, he is deep inside the rock; again, his flame burns much lower than it did. This world is getting older; the elemental forces and the spirits, some of them not good, which clustered about them are guttering out. He had a voice once; now he can only pull to himself a few half-lost souls. This is his danger to your brother, for whatever happened to you has happened so much more strongly to him that he has room for nothing else. The black desire has him very tight. See how he fears to look at me?'

Andrew's contorted face stared towards the ground: he was twisted so that his back was turned mainly towards them. He remained passive and motionless. He had his hands over his ears.

'Andrew!' cried Laura. 'Oh, why has he become like this? And why him and not me? Why didn't it work properly on me, is it because I'm thicker-souled and have less imagination? I always thought imagination a good thing, yet I know this enchantment is bad for Andrew – oh, I don't understand it!'

'It's not simply a matter of the imagination,' came the reply, only it was getting harder to understand what was said through the roaring noise of water. 'The enchanter has played upon and intensified desires and memories which are in every mortal being. You are neither less nor more clever or imaginative than he; you were lucky, nothing else, in escaping. Chance has always its part to play. It was probably some quite technical error on the enchanter's part that he didn't win you, too. You may have been in the wrong position; Andrew's body may have blocked you out. You may have had an instinctive resistance right from the start which was just enough to protect you.'

'Oh, I see,' said Laura, relieved. It had been very wounding to her pride to feel in some way that she might not have had the imagination to qualify for enchantment, unpleasant though its consequences undoubtedly were. It had spoiled her whole conception of herself so that she now didn't know what kind of person she was supposed to be. But perhaps fortunately she had had little time to brood on this, she had been so taken up with her concern for Andrew. Poor Andrew, what bad luck it had been for him! She turned to try to see his face and as she relaxed her hold he made an eel-like movement and was free of her, clambering over the stones across a narrow part of the stream as it collected its forces again after the wide pool made by the waterfall.

'Stop him, by any means,' cried the woman urgently through the noise of the water, and now the water and the light seemed to fall between her and Laura. 'He *must* not get to the top or he is lost!'

'Why, what will happen?' cried Laura, clutching literally at her heart through which a great stab of fear had pierced.

'Don't you know? Don't you know where he's making for? He's going up along High Scar Edge to the end, to throw himself off Stony Head Pike. The fall will kill him, for the watcher who dwells there will see to that and he will belong to the enchanter for ever: or at least until this world's end.'

'Oh, my golly,' said Laura weakly. She took a step and then looked back. It was at this moment that she had a most unpleasant experience. As if she had previously been wrapped in a layer of cotton wool or a kind of cocoon she almost physically felt a rending and a lifting of some protective covering about her, and a piercing shaft of light flooded in which turned everything about her grey and lifeless in contrast. She tried to look through the light which had come between her and the woman to whom she had been speaking, and it so hurt her eyes that she had to turn away. She had a fleeting impression of being watched by many faces; more cruel and malign than before, they clustered about her, waiting, watching hopefully, and she found herself compelled to look upwards in the direction of the hills where a spirit of great power dwelt. And now she felt the full force of the watcher's evil attraction, he was killing all normal human feeling within her, and she began to understand that for her there were now no pleasant sounds left on earth; nothing to see, for the colour had drained from the sky; no pleasure in eating or drinking, for the taste in her mouth would be dust.

She feared to go onward yet there was nothing else to do: the black, salty itch to climb upon his rock face, to cast herself forward and down, to know herself as herself no longer – to be a *thing* crawling under the monstrous no-face of One; poked and prodded and counted by the gloating, complacent half-human Other: this had become her desire, the only desire left to her: the only desire worth desiring.

There was something resembling a snap inside her head, almost as if a wire had pulled out or a faulty connection broken loose. Laura, dazed for a moment, staggered into the stream so that one foot was soaked. She gasped at the shock of the cold water and normality returned. There was no sign of any woman near or far. The waterfall was an ordinary waterfall with no odd light effects. The sky above her was prosaically clouding over. She could hear Andrew scrambling over rocks somewhere on a higher level above her and above the waterfall. She must follow him, though the tops of the hills which were hidden to her in this valley exerted now no fascination, no lure. Whatever there had been of enchantment for her was now over; she had finally broken away. But there remained the hard, inescapable fact of Andrew's continued enchantment, and now she understood only too well the strength of the powers that bound him.

The path turned away from the waterfall and was obviously going to make a detour through the trees. But he had gone straight up, over the rocks. So Laura followed him, slipping and slithering over the stones and found herself quickly out of the wood, in a long, slanting valley. It narrowed further on and the stream disappeared into another group of trees which came down to meet it on either side. Andrew had already nearly reached the trees and as she found level grass again and was able to run, he disappeared from view. It was getting grey all about her; grey and chilly and shaping up for rain. A sodden lump of something that proved to be a long-dead lamb lay in the water halfway up. She averted her eyes and ran on.

It was gloomy under the next group of trees, in contrast to the pleasant places lower down. The ground sloped here very steeply on either side away from the stream and the trees were mostly evergreen, fir and a few pine. One had an enclosed feeling: the narrow path was dark and gloomy and smelt of wild garlic of which, together with waist-high nettles, there was an abundance. Also both sheep and cows and possibly some other animals had been up this way not so very long ago and their dung was everywhere, so that Laura had to watch carefully where she put her feet. The roar of the lower waterfall had died away long ago but now she became aware of another, louder roar; there must be another fall higher up. It began to rain, and although she was reasonably well protected by the trees, every now and then a spot fell on her and made her uneasily aware how inadequate her clothing was for bad weather. She was wearing a cotton skirt and blouse with a light cardigan, white socks to the knee and her white plimsolls were already soaked and dark with mud.

'I don't like this place,' she muttered to herself to keep her courage up by the sound of a human voice. 'And Andrew, where are you? I wish I could see you.'

She stopped to listen but there was nothing but the sound of water and no sign of him. She rounded the next corner and there, down precipitous slopes, one of the longest waterfalls she had ever seen fell with a slow thunder. She was out of sight of most of the pool it made though she could see it was possible to scramble down in one place to it. The path stopped among the rocks and as far as she could see did not go any farther. There was no possible way up by the waterfall itself, it was too steep; a dangerous, nasty, frightening place, and the smell of mud and water and garlic became overpowering and she shuddered as she almost put her foot in a great horrible gobbet of dung.

Then Laura's eye was caught by something moving high

above and to one side of her, up the steep slope of evergreens which clustered so thickly down to this waterfall. It was Andrew, scrambling on hands and knees, pulling himself by roots and branches up and up. It was the only possible way to go if one did not retrace one's steps. This was obviously the head of this particular dale: the waterfall must be Ramshead Force: above and beyond this must be the open moors and Firedale Forest which was now open land without a single tree, just as her father had shown it to her on the map.

Without any further hesitation Laura began the upward climb. It would be a relief to get out of this place; anywhere was better than here where she felt the trees drawing in on her, where the constant noise confused and weakened her, where the slow continual falling, falling of the water sought to pull her down. A bad place: if there was or had been a watcher here he was evil; he was to be shunned. This she would have known without ever having been enchanted, any sensitive person could know it.

Soon the waterfall was a confused noise and memory below her, as she forced her labouring body to climb the steep slope, muddying her clothes and her arms and legs as she slipped and slithered and hauled herself up. Suddenly she was beyond the tree line and it was all different again.

She was on the bare open moors. There was no sign of the top because it was hidden by a shoulder of heather and peat. Distances were deceptive up here and the rain came driving down in sheets into her face. The clouds were low and dark grey and she could not see very far in any direction. Andrew was about a quarter of a mile ahead of her: there was no path here and he was striking straight up over the bog cotton and among the peat hags and the little hidden tarns.

Because it was easier to see about her and she had got away from the claustrophobic valley with its waterfall, Laura felt a little better and easier in her mind. The distance between them was diminishing slightly, too: it looked as though Andrew were limping slightly, and floundering, and this cheered her. She did not realize at this stage that, soaked almost to the skin, exposed in light clothing to wind and rain, she and Andrew were both in growing danger. Why, it was summer, it could not be so very cold and a little rain could be nothing more than unpleasant – could it?

Laura breasted the slope and then found a wild and lonely moor which stretched to the foot of the crags and rocks that gave High Scar Edge its name. The low-lying cloud only just cleared the top. It was a barren, formidable place, whether there was anything watching up there or not; in a sense it was all watching her; now she had lost her perception of one particular presence in the stone. About the moor were littered what at first she took for large stones but which proved to be sheep. They were scattering everywhere as Andrew stumbled through them.

'Baa – aagh.' A low gutteral sound at one side made her jump as a large grey ewe with torn, filthy wool and two half-grown lambs at her side leapt suddenly to her feet and ran hastily off, the lambs close behind her wagging their tails in fright.

'Ughh': another low-pitched bubbling grunt at her other side, a sound as far removed from the high-pitched innocent baa of a young lamb as it is possible to imagine. Some ancient weatherbeaten grandmother of the hills this, and her hugeness and her dirty hanks of hair and her staring yellow eyes made Laura remember her vision and the question she had answered: *the souls of the enchanted are in the sheep.* These must be they: these were the flock of Firedale Forest. And yet she couldn't entirely believe it now: now the vision had departed. Surely they were just *sheep*? Why, this next half-grown lamb that bolted almost under her feet and waddled awkwardly with fright and surprise as it ran, this could only be pure animal? But although thoughts such as these went to and fro in Laura's mind, and she doubted herself, and what she was trying to do, she kept doggedly on and on and feared she now knew not what. And she hardly realized the growing numbness of her hands and the way she was slowing up and tending to stumble over the smallest roughness in the ground.

A long time went by, and another slow mile of difficult ground covered. Both Andrew and Laura were now travelling very slowly, panting and often stumbling. Physical wretchedness began to overwhelm Laura. It was difficult to think of anything much when one was feeling like this; and in this at least the weather was merciful to her, for it killed most of the fear and anxiety she might otherwise have experienced. This is the true experience of much heroic endeavour, for Laura's endeavour was indeed heroic: there was no excitement to it, no thrill of danger and knowledge of life lived to the utmost, there was just the miserable cold and wet and the slow forcing of her staggering body onwards. As for her mind, it hardly existed.

'Oh!'

She had been so preoccupied with laborious climbing from one peat hag to another that she had temporarily forgotten the figure ahead: now it wavered with a cry of surprise and pain, and sat down almost out of sight in the heather.

He was crying when at last she reached him.

'Oh Laura, it hurts so! I can't, I can't!' Andrew didn't often cry and Laura noticed with relief that, as before, his physical hurt appeared, temporarily at least, to shock him partially out of his enchantment and he would talk to her.

'I've hurt my foot so: it twisted under this root.'

'Andrew, it's beastly up here,' cried Laura through chattering teeth. 'Lean on me or something and we'll go back. There's no protection from the wind. And I'm soaked right through to my tummy. I'll get pneumonia or something.'

'I can't. I've *got* to go on.'

'You mustn't, you mustn't. Don't you understand, you'll be killed! That's what he wants.'

'I can't help it. I have to – you don't know what it's like. There's no escaping him, he's twisting my brain tighter and

86

tighter. I'm squeezing dry, Laura, there'll be nothing left of me soon!'

'We *must* get *off* here,' cried Laura, looking wildly around. 'Come on, there's some broken stones or something. We'll sit there, it'll get us out of this horrible wind a bit.'

A mound of stones nearby showed that they were near one of the deserted lead mines. They were partly fallen in and filled with water and Laura shuddered in sympathy with those long-ago men who had had to work down the mean little tunnels in this grim, desolating place, so high and exposed to bad weather. There was no romance to the word 'lead mine' now; it was a different, more foolish Laura who had had those imaginings at the beginning of the holiday. There could be no buried treasure up here; just the faint memory of men forced to labour to the limit of their endurance for long, cold hours day after day, year in, year out.

Laura and Andrew sat silent for a while, huddled together in the lee of the largest heap of broken stones. The rain was temporarily slackening, and a few rifts appearing in the layers of cloud overhead. For a few seconds a yellow shaft of sunlight pierced through, turning the colour of the heavy clouds over the tops of the hills slate blue and the grass and rocks tawny. About a quarter of a mile away, under the cliff edge, Laura saw a big ram picked out by the light, his horned head carried high, and he seemed to be looking directly at her. Then the sun went in and the rain dashed down again and it became grey and featureless and difficult to see. Was he a magical beast? Had she really seen him?

Turning her head from the rain in bewilderment, Laura remembered she had half a bar of chocolate in her pocket. She ate a mouthful herself and then offered it to Andrew. He was too cold and far gone to take it: he sat hunched miserably, shivering and shivering. She had never seen him look so white; his eyes were half shut and the sight of him shocked her into further activity.

'Come on, wake up, you must have this,' she cried, breaking the chocolate into small pieces and stuffing it into his mouth so that he was forced to chew it. 'It'll give you energy. Oh, how can I help you when you don't help yourself?'

As she pushed the last piece into his open, chattering jaws, she was reminded of a time when she had once had to feed a baby thrush with worms. It had fallen early from its nest and was scuffling pathetically round the garden, quite unable to fly. They had captured it and put it in the shed and dug up bloated, earthy, wriggling horrors for it, and then had to stuff them far back into its gaping beak before the ridiculous creature would swallow. Andrew, in his helplessness was almost like that bird, except that it was better to thrust chocolate into a mouth than worms. It had survived two days and then had been caught by a cat, so all their hard work was wasted.

The few pieces of chocolate were gone. She looked up and *there*, as a particularly vicious spurt of wind-borne rain dashed into her face, half blinding her, *there* suddenly from nowhere, a monstrous, humped creature loomed over the heather: a two-legged, armless, faceless, swollen horror. It was coming towards them, a man-beast from the hills; it had all been true, there had been something up there after all . . .

Laura's scream raised a curlew from the other side of the mines, and as it flapped slowly away, it echoed her cry with a call so piercingly wild and plaintive that it seemed to contain within it all the mystery and loneliness of the bare hilltops which surrounded them. But Laura, who had wished so ardently to commune with Nature, did not hear it. She had her head buried in her arms, crouching blind and deaf, helpless as any little cornered animal.

# eleven

'Another buttered teacake, darling?'

'Yes, all right,' said Laura, taking two. She leant back blissfully in her chair before the fire, putting her mug of hot cocoa carefully down on the fender.

'I'm not really all that hungry now, but I just like going on eating.'

'I'm sure you need it,' said her mother. 'I'll boil you another egg or two, if you'd like.'

'You know,' exclaimed Laura, her mouth full and feeling very pleasantly relaxed and talkative, 'you know, there's nothing nicer than doing something really *horrid* and getting just as cold and soaked to the skin as possible, and rather frightened as well, because then it is all over and one can get all dry and warm and think how beastly it was outside and feel so thankful to be out of it. Listen to the rain now! I'd *die* if I were out in it again.'

'Indeed you're nearer the truth than you think,' said the holidaying schoolmaster who had found Laura and Andrew and brought them down. It was he whose sudden appearance had so terrified Laura. He had been walking, hooded head bent against the rain, arms hunched to his chest, large knapsack upon his back, upon a path which led from the top to the lead mines and thence by slow undulations and half-circles down again, avoiding the highest waterfall to join the lush, cow-spattered meadows below the second waterfall. And so when he saw the two of them and their condition (he had to shake Laura before she would raise her head and look at him), he took off his anorak and wrapped it round Andrew, found a sweater in his knapsack and gave it to Laura, hid the knapsack itself under a rock to be fetched the next day, piggybacked Andrew in its place (luckily he was the tough, athletic kind of schoolmaster) and by exhortation and admonishment brought the stumbling, exhausted Laura in his wake, down, down at last to the blessed fire and food and comfort.

Andrew, too exhausted to protest, had been put to bed with two hot water bottles.

'Indeed I wonder whether we ought not to have a doctor out to have a look at him?' Mrs Hearst had said.

'I shouldn't think there's anything wrong with him that rest and warmth won't cure,' his father had said. 'As long as he's really warm now.'

They decided that he was all right, and he very quickly went to sleep, looking pink and flushed and with his mouth open. The schoolmaster was given a hot drink by the fire and thanked again and again.

'I won't say I'm not glad of a bit of a rest before going on down to the village where we're staying,' he said. 'Your son isn't all that big for his age fortunately, but he's made of good solid stuff, all right. He seemed to get heavier and heavier. Still, we managed.'

'I reckon you might well have saved those children's lives,' said Laura's father. 'Naturally, we can't thank you enough. And of course we'd no idea they'd got so far up on the moors. High Scar Edge is some miles from here and it's difficult going. I suppose a few people must walk that way in good weather, but it must be deserted for days on end in bad.'

'Yes, what a blessing you were walking just there at that time,' exclaimed Mrs Hearst.

'It was,' returned the schoolmaster shortly.

'Oh well, all's well that end's well. But Laura, *never never* go for a walk in bad weather dressed like that again. And don't go so far, darling, without us.'

'It was Andrew wanted to,' explained Laura to her mother. 'I was trying to make him come down.'

'Well, I think Andrew must have taken leave of his senses. Ron and Cath were a bit worried about you too – the way you rushed off and the time you both were. They stayed awhile and then they had to go off to their supper. We weren't back until after seven ourselves, you see, and we heard you'd been gone since about four.'

'I was just going to turn out again to look for them, though I was pretty tired from going up the Pennine Way, when I saw you with them,' said Laura's father to the schoolmaster. 'The trouble is one doesn't know where to begin to look ... there's a lot of country out there.'

'Could we really have *died*?' asked Laura as the full importance of what had happened struck her anew. 'We were miserably cold and wet but when the rain stopped I was going to go down for help, at least I think I was ...'

'Ever heard of something called cold exhaustion?' asked the schoolmaster. 'If your body gets below a certain temperature you could well never recover. It doesn't need ice or snow: rain and cold wind can be just as deadly. I should think that Andrew at any rate was very near to that condition. As for you, it would have been a matter of time. If the bad weather had continued you might well have died of exposure by the next morning. I've had some experience of taking parties of children up on the moors, you see, and know it must be done properly.'

'Oo.' Laura wriggled luxuriously inside her warmest jersey. The moor was very far away now: everything was. Now she had got Andrew down and he had a day or so in bed, surely her task was over? Her mind sheered away from enchantment, away from Mr Strange, away from the continuance of the bad dream she had been living. She had endured so much: she deserved that it should be over. There would be no further trial. When Andrew recovered from the effects of his exposure and twisted ankle he would be back to normal. Surely.

'I do understand that it was mainly Andrew's fault,' said her mother suddenly, who had been watching her.

'Laura did very well,' put in the schoolmaster. 'Better than lots of kids I know. I'm sorry if I bullied you, Laura, coming down, but I had to. I just had to get you along for your own sake. We were very dependent on those legs of yours not giving out: I couldn't have carried both of you. And now I'd better be getting back to my own family or they'll be worried.'

'I'll pop you down in the car.' Mr Hearst went out with him, thanking him all over again, and Laura fell comfortably asleep in her chair.

Clink, clank, a cow bellowing somewhere in the distance, morning smells, a sudden feeling one must get up.

'Hello, I've brought your milk down,' called a voice.

Ann's pink jolly face was upturned to Laura as she looked out of the window. The clock on the window-sill said half past eight.

'Doing anything today?' asked Ann hopefully. 'Like to come and help me drive the cows back?'

Laura stretched and considered. She was tired and stiff but not excessively so.

'OK. I'll have to get some clothes on.'

'No hurry. I'll wait then. What about Andrew?'

'Oh, not him. He slept in my parents' room last night. We moved a bed in. He hurt his ankle and I should think he'll have to rest today.'

In about five minutes' time Laura, munching an apple for breakfast, was walking through the wet grass with Ann. It was a grey and windy day: not yet settled after the rain. It was a relief to Laura, after all she had been through, to be with a girl of her own age, and someone so pleasant and undemanding as Ann.

'They're up in the little yard by the barn,' Ann said. 'I've to take them down the road and on to the field at t'corner.'

The twenty or so cows awaited them, mostly black and white, mild and inquiring, blowing great grassy breaths at them.

'I'll lead the way,' said Ann obligingly. 'You can follow them. You and our dog.'

A black and white sheepdog emerged from a shed and ran obsequiously up to Laura, wagging its tail.

'Hey up, girls.'

The procession slowly sorted itself out and got under way. It gave Laura a pleasant feeling of power to strut behind, although the movement was slow and she had to watch where she put her feet. There were many good reasons for being thickly shod in this countryside.

When the cows had been finally shut into their field and were dispersing gradually down one side of it eating as they went, Ann and Laura leant pensively against the gate watching them.

'It was odd that old fellow not being there,' said Ann suddenly.

Laura knew exactly to whom she was referring. 'Do you think he's gone away for good?' she said cautiously. It was her hope, but it seemed too good to be true.

'Mother and me came to the conclusion he was just a tramp camping out there who got scared and went off,' said Ann. 'Mother said you could tell the police if you wanted. Father didn't say anything to that but then he never does. We don't reckon Mrs Anderson knew anything about him after all.'

'No,' said Laura thoughtfully. If only he *had* gone; if only she could get him out of her mind!

'If you were in a fairy tale and had to find a great singing beast with talking wings, what would you do?' she asked suddenly, almost in spite of herself.

'Whatever do you mean? Get over Bessie, do.' (This was to the dog who was sitting scratching herself on Ann's feet.)

There was a silence. 'Wait,' said Ann with a sudden giggle.

'What?'

'You've given me an idea, that's all. Will you be around after dinner sometime? I'll bring something to show you. That'll give you a surprise that will.'

'What?' asked Laura.

'It's a surprise,' returned Ann and would say no more.

They walked back up the road, could think of nothing

more to do together or say to each other and so parted company, and Ann went home over the stile to her mother.

And so it was that Laura was alone when she saw him, standing under the signpost on the crossroads above the lake, standing still, his hands clasped upon his crook and smiling at her.

'You needn't think you have changed anything, you know,' he said gently. 'You have only won yourself a little time. When he has eaten and slept again and the swelling in his foot is better, I shall tighten my grip once more, for I hold him like that in the palm of my hand.'

And he raised his so clean, manicured fingers to her and rubbed and squeezed them across his palm as if he were crumbling bread.


## twelve


In the afternoon the sun came out and stayed out. That made it better. Also there was the bustle of bidding goodbye to Ron and Cath. Laura was sorry to see them go, although her mother obviously was not. They had breakfasted late, after the Hearst family; a large fry-up of eggs and bacon, and had been rather messy and underfoot in the kitchen, and absolutely and cheerfully unaware of it. Today Cath wore a long cotton skirt which reached to her bare, sandalled feet. Ron had a deep V-necked shirt which showed more of his hairy chest than ever.

'Whatever made you and Andrew go so far up the moors anyway?' Ron asked Laura through a mouthful of bacon. 'And you hared off so suddenly too, as if you were practising for a cross-country race or something. Ann went a bit of the way after you when you'd been gone about ten minutes or so, to see if she could see you, but she came back and reported total disappearance.'

Laura made some non-committal answer and to her relief Ron did not pursue the subject, merely crunching up more bacon with gusto. He had overcooked it terribly, filling the kitchen with smoke and spitting fat.

'I've never been upon the moors at all,' said Cath, 'apart from driving over them. I don't like them. Bleak, nothing to draw.'

'You don't like walking, you mean. You'd be frightened your legs would drop off.'

'There's not much sense in endlessly putting one foot in front of the other, it's so tiring,' returned Cath, running her fingers through her hair, to comb it.

And that was the end of that conversation. Ron went outside to poke timelessly within the bonnet of his car and Cath returned to complete her drawing until they suddenly decided that they had better get going. Mr and Mrs Hearst and Laura went outside to bid them farewell.

'It was nice meeting you all,' said Ron heartily, as he swung their two sleeping bags into the back of the car. 'I'll give your regards to Jimmy, I'll be seeing him tonight. I'm sure he'll be glad to hear you've settled in so well here and are having a good time. I hope Andrew's ankle is better soon and you don't have any more trouble from that old tramp in the loft or whatever he was. But he doesn't seem to be there now, does he? I had a good look yesterday, but there's no trace of him.'

Cath packed up her drawing and climbed in beside Ron. 'Goodbye,' she said, smiling faintly.

'Goodbye!'

'Goodbye, have a pleasant drive,' called Mrs Hearst, in whose hearty tones relief at their going was more noticeable than any real concern as to their welfare. But Laura ran up the drive after them and watched the little red sports car disappear down the hill and round the corner, then reappear up the next hill much smaller in size, with only the faintest noise of its engine, then disappear for good over the crest of the hill. They had gone: she would not see them again.

Silence. Nobody driving or walking past: nothing happening. Her father and mother had disappeared somewhere; her father most probably to go fishing. A thick depression began to blanket her about: a slow lethargic listlessness and feeling that nothing was of any use. For Mr Strange had *not* gone, however empty the loft might appear to be. There was no more she could do, and anyway she was too tired and fed up to care.

'Hey!' called a voice. 'Hey! Laura! Come and see what I've got here.'

Laura roused herself from her melancholy reflections and looked over the wall and saw walking along the path in the next field a short, thickset figure. Ann. She was carrying something on her arm: something that flapped.

'Isn't he a beauty!' she cried as she came a little nearer. 'I told you I'd a surprise for you. Something you said just put me in mind of him.'

'Good gracious,' said Laura weakly, as Ann came up to her. 'It's a parrot.'

A grey and red parrot perched on Ann's arm. He looked at Laura steadily and blinked his eye once. ' 'Ello,' he said putting his head on one side. ' 'Ello, 'ello 'ello.'

'Hello, parrot,' Laura replied. She felt she ought to continue the conversation, he had looked at her with such a very knowing, sophisticated eye, but then he suddenly lost interest in a very inhuman way and began to trample up and down on Ann's arm and burrow his head under his wing.

Ann looked at Laura's face and burst out laughing.

'I couldn't resist bringing him to see you after all that you said about a pair of talking wings. He's a pair of talking wings all right, isn't he?'

'Yes,' agreed Laura, her depression lifting a little. She had not thought of a parrot, and although there still was and still could not be a great singing beast ... yet she had not thought of a parrot, and here of all unlikely things in this dale, was a parrot.

'Where did you get him? Does he say anything else? What's his name?'

It appeared that his name was Freddy. 'And he says quite a bit,' said Ann looking at him proudly as if she were his mother. ' " 'Bye bye" . . . as well as "hello", and "good boy" and "good night" – and oh – lots else.'

'Freddy? Freddy?' tried Laura, meeting his aged, this-time unblinking gaze. He held up one claw a moment to her and then slowly lowered it, keeping his eyes fixed on her face.

'See, he likes you,' said Ann. 'Give him a nut.'

She burrowed in her pocket with her free hand and produced a walnut.

'He's not yours? Surely?' asked Laura, proffering the nut. 'Oh, I wish I had a parrot.'

'No,' giggled Ann regretfully. 'But I *am* allowed to take him out for a walk as he's so tame and good. But I've never taken him as far as this. He lives in the big house a mile back. Before the village. My auntie's housekeeper there and Mrs Harte, the owner, is away now so auntie let me borrow him. I'd better take him back soon. Shall I just show him to your mother and father? And Andrew? My little brother won't touch him. He's scared. But then Andrew's much older.'

Ann began to climb over the wall, the parrot balancing on her shoulder.

'Andrew's still in bed—' Laura was beginning, when Ann interrupted her. She sat down on the wall and jerked her head sideways. 'Did you hear that bellow? That's our bull. Father and two of the men from Hayter's farm are bringing him down, and he's an awkward one. Father wanted John to help too, that's my big brother, but he's gone off with his girl friend somewhere.'

There was another bellow and the sound of running feet and indistinct shouts.

'He's coming down now,' said Ann, pivoting round to watch.

At a slow canter round the corner came a bull; looking excited and cross, two men with pitchforks on either side of him, another behind.

'Watch it!' cried Ann suddenly. 'Someone's coming up.'

A confused murmur of tinny sound; high pseudo-American voices chanting, electric guitars twanging, all this impinged upon the ear from the road just below them and there slowly ambled into view Ann's big brother, John, carrying that proof of courtship, a transistor radio, dangling from a strap from one hand; the other hand held the hand of a dark bosomy girl Laura had noticed once in a cottage garden in the village below. They came full upon the bull who was now at full gallop and out-distancing his guards. It all happened just by the wall on which Ann was sitting and Laura leaning. There was a confused mêlée of shouts and screams, then the bull swerved through the only open way left to him, straight through the open gate through which Laura had seen Ron and Cath's car depart, through the gate and down the rough drive towards Ramshead Lodge. But there was something odd about the bull. Something had caught on his horn and was bumping against his head and annoying him. Yet he did not pause but cantered straight on, pursued now for some reason by no one; except Laura and the parrot.

For the parrot with a great shriek had raised itself from Ann's shoulder and flown off. It was all so quick that Laura hardly knew what was happening except that Andrew, as if on cue, appeared at the front door of the house still in his pyjamas, a dazed look upon his face. Laura had no time to cry out, because at that moment, at the sight of Andrew, the bull swerved, turned sideways towards the stables, cantered along the path and halted at the stable steps, shaking his head in bewilderment. A thin half-broken noise of singing was still to be heard from the transistor whose strap had somehow become attached to the bull's horn and the parrot for some reason best known to itself (perhaps it thought the bull had impaled some strange other kind of parrot upon its horn) fluttered round the bull's head, buffeting the unfortunate animal about the eyes with its wings, and shrieking out 'Naughty boy!' as if it had been wound up and could not stop.

Mr Strange was standing at the head of the stable steps. And so it was Laura who came up to him, and so excited at what had happened in such a swift and unexpected fashion that she had no fear of the bull, she called out in what breath she had left: 'The magic of chance, the magic of chance! It's the great singing beast with the talking wings, Mr Strange. They *have* come together and they *do* rebuke you, so what can you do now Mr Strange?'

'Naughty boy!' shrieked the parrot, leaving the bull and flying wildly about. 'Naughty boy! Naughty boy!'

He stood and Laura saw something leave him. It was as if he crumpled. He said not a word but went inside and shut the door.

Meanwhile events began to relax and unwind in a perfectly normal and natural manner. The bull, seeing the lower stable door open, trotted meekly inside to its comforting darkness and the first of the men with pitchforks (they had all stumbled and fallen over each other at the gate) arriving at this minute was able to clap the door shut after him. The parrot, obviously out of breath, fluttered back to the horrified Ann who began to soothe him, and tucking him under her arm disappeared rapidly over the fields with him.

John now appeared bewailing his transistor at last flung to the ground and trampled.

'The b—' he kept saying, 'got my radio from me just like that. Just with one swoop.'

'Lucky he didn't get you,' said his father sourly. '*And* we shouldn't have had this trouble if you'd been with us. Y' know it takes four of us to handle him.'

Laura sat down and began to laugh. She laughed and laughed until she ached. It was partly hysteria, she knew.

After a little more talk and with the help of John (his girl friend had tactfully disappeared), the four men together manoeuvred the now much calmer bull out of the stable and to the field he was meant to be in, and silence gradually fell. Andrew remained at the doorway, in his pyjamas, looking calmly and placidly out, as though nothing had happened.

'Are you all right, Andrew?' asked Laura at last. He must be: he must be: the enchanter had to keep his word, they always did for some reason, she knew that.

'All right,' he replied willingly enough but on the wrong note, a mere echo.

'Andrew!'

She ran over and looked at him. The frantic look had left him certainly, there had been a change, but what was this pleasant, inane little smile doing on his lips? It wasn't *Andrew*, it was not his habit to smile like that.

'Do you feel all right, Andrew?' she asked again.

'Feel all right,' he echoed her, still smiling. It was as if he were half-broken: as if something in him had run down. It was dreadful.

But Laura had the confidence of the incredible having already happened: she could not be balked now.

'Come with me,' she said, and she led Andrew along the side of the house and up the steps and she knocked at Mr Strange's door.

Her last trial and battle with him was yet to come.

# thirteen

Laura knocked again at the door at the top of the steps. Both halves were closed. A long silence had followed her first two knocks, and with a sudden surge of fear she knocked a third time, loudly.

'All right, all right,' came an irritated voice from within. 'Can't you let me alone in peace to do my packing?'

The top half swung open and there inside Laura saw him wrapping one of his many china ornaments carefully in tissue paper. A great mess of packing cases and more paper and straw lay about him. It seemed, with such a wealth of things about the room, impossible that she could have seen it bare and empty only the day before.

'You see, I am going,' he said. 'Surely it is bad enough, my having to leave my little house in which I'd been so happy without you coming to gloat over me, you horrible girl.'

'I'm sorry,' said Laura blankly. She did not know what she had visualized at the end of the enchantment; certainly not this. It is one thing to justly defeat an enemy; it is quite another to witness the pathetic consequences of that defeat. Besides, he looked so natural, so normal; he had always looked so natural, so normal. Just a fashionably dressed country gentleman with artistic leanings, likeable and chatty, if a little petulant at times. Even now, after all that had happened, it was possible to doubt oneself. What had she done to him? Could she be all mixed up and wrong?

'Oh dear,' exclaimed Mr Strange sadly. 'And now I've broken the head off one of my cherubs.'

He tossed a broken piece of china upon the floor. Somehow this seemed to be Laura's fault too.

'But it isn't!' she suddenly burst out. She remembered Andrew and her resolution and indignation strengthened. 'I don't understand, but I suppose it is a part of your beastly magic; if you can make your room empty so swiftly when you please, there's no *need* for all this fuss over packing, surely!'

Mr Strange shot her a venomous glance but said nothing and continued to rustle among his tissue paper. Laura opened the door wide.

'You can't leave Andrew like this,' she cried, pointing to him as he sat smiling at the bottom of the steps. 'He's still not right. He's got to be returned exactly as he was before he met you.'

'Met you,' echoed Andrew, looking up, his mouth open.

'You see.' Laura gestured towards him.

'Of course I see. What *more* can you want of me? You're driving me from my little home. I've broken the lovely, lovely enchantment for you so that he doesn't want to go up the hill and visit my friend and join my little flock, such a waste when I'd got so far with him; absolutely ripe, he was. *Just* the way I like them.'

'What more do I want?' said Laura helplessly. It was upside down: it was so unfair that she should have to argue with him like this, that he should try to put *her* in the wrong.

She had a very strong desire to burst into tears – indeed screams of rage and frustration, but somehow she controlled herself, knowing that it would do her cause harm rather than good. As steadily as she could she said again: 'I have answered your questions. You must make Andrew right.'

Mr Strange wiped his hands on a duster. 'I think you are very narrow-minded,' he said. 'How can you tell that the course I had planned for him wasn't the best thing that could happen to him? You have spoiled all that and what right had you to do it? What is so wrong with him now? He looks happy enough.'

'Happy,' returned Andrew, laughing at nothing.

'You see I suppose I *could* put him in a sleep of forget-fulness but it would be the most awful effort for me, so tiring and weakening: *just* when I needed a little more nourishment, a little more sustenance. I'm not a young man, Laura, you must consider me a little, but you young people are all the same.'

'A sleep of forgetfulness,' Laura said as firmly as she was able. 'You mean he will forget the whole enchantment: forget he ever met you; be just as he was before.'

'Something like that,' returned Mr Strange shortly.

'Then you must do it, you've got to do it.'

He came out and faced her. Laura's legs trembled. What could he do to her? But then she saw his eyes waver, the corners of his lips drop. A tear trickled slowly down his nose, and she suddenly realized that because of what had happened she had the ascendancy over him, she really could make him do as she wished; she could, if she had the resolution, hold him to his bargain. She heard again the woman by the waterfall say 'You must be firm.' And now she understood what she had meant.

'Put Andrew in a sleep of forgetfulness,' she ordered.

He mopped his eye with a silk handkerchief and appeared to pull himself together.

'Let us go down into the meadow,' he said. 'Follow me, please, both of you.'

They walked a little way through the long grasses, Andrew following them, sweeping his hand over their feathery tops and giggling to himself.

'There, behind the brambles,' said Mr Strange softly.

Behind the brambles sat the cat, William. He had a very dead mouse between his paws, as if to encourage it into motion again.

'He's a clever cat, a good hunter,' said Mr Strange. 'It is his nature. He needs to hunt to live. I, also. I need people – to do things with, to count, to enjoy. It's my nature. You can't blame me, I was made like that. You wouldn't want to spoil William's life for him, why should you wish to spoil my life? Without anybody I dry up, crack and wither. It is most unfair and cruel and narrow of you, Laura.'

'Put Andrew in a sleep of forgetfulness.' Laura's voice

rose and she clenched her fists: it was all she could do to withstand him.

He took no notice of her, but continued in a voice of the most perfect sweetness and reasonableness. 'And are you really considering your brother, Andrew? If he forgets and goes back to normal, he may have a far unhappier life than he would have done if he had dwelt, as it were, under my wing. You ordinary mortals don't always have such easy lives, you know. Andrew may be disappointed and thwarted at every turn. He may marry a shrewish wife. He might have an unpleasant, dull, grinding job. How can you condemn him to all that?'

Oh, the pure unfairness of it! That he should use such weapons against her! Might he not be right? Andrew looked happy enough now; he wasn't always happy as his ordinary self, he fought with boys at scool, he hated French, he had heavy colds and tonsillitis every winter. Laura suddenly felt tired, fed up with all the responsibility, she wanted to run away, to say, 'Very well, do as you like. I don't care. You can count me out.' But then a memory came to her, for no particular reason. She remembered his last birthday present to her. Sometimes they didn't much bother with each other's birthdays, but last time he'd not only saved his money and managed to get her a paperback book she especially wanted, but contrived to keep it a secret from her so that it should be a good surprise on the morning. She remembered how it had sat, beautifully wrapped, upon her plate and how he made her open it before all her other presents and how he had been so pleased at her surprise he had run out of the room laughing. That had been a pleasant time: for him not to be ordinary and happy like that and for them not to have fun together was unthinkable. She did not always like her brother, but she loved him and occasionally she both liked and loved him.

And so she said again for the third time as strongly as she could:

'Put Andrew in a sleep of forgetfulness.'

She was never sure exactly what happened next. For a few seconds there was a great noise because every creature within a mile or so gave tongue, the cows mooed, the far-distant bull bellowed, the ponies from the pony-trekking farm whinnied, dogs barked, there was the far-off bray of a donkey, birds croaked, chirped and chattered and there was, from the hills all about them, an endless baa-ing of sheep. William, the cat, yowled and Mr Strange threw back his head and shocked Laura immensely by giving the most blood-curdling wolvish howl she had ever heard from man or beast. It sent cold shivers down her spine. Then he bent over in a terrible way and began to gabble at her, his face working and altering most horribly:

'I must have him, don't you see I must have someone, half a person is better than none, something, anything, my thirst is such, don't you understand, without someone to feed me I don't exist. I go, I'm nothing—' and as these words left his mouth the horrified Laura saw upon his now no-longer pleasant face the expression and likeness of many kinds of animals: a malign monkey face, the watchful self-absorption of a cat, a hungry wolf: he had the cold eye of a reptile, the snarl of a tiger and as she watched and understood the likeness of human to animal and animal to human his face changed purely to human again as if as a human he could in fact reach lower depths of bestiality and rapacity than any animal. He was eaten-up with self-regard, the flesh pulling away from the naked skull that now left a hollow nothing-face with two gaping eyes and a clenched grin of teeth. This creature of bent bone twitched, clutched at her and finally fell, brittle as a skeleton, at her feet. It was as if he were made of nothing: all skins peeled off like an onion, he had no central core.

But Laura had no time to do more than stare in frozen horror because the very next moment, as if nothing had happened, the impeccable Mr Strange, in full possession of every faculty, his pink, smooth cheeks full, his white hair carefully waved and brushed, got to his feet, dusted down his trousers and took Andrew's head between his hands.

'I hear and obey you,' he said in his old gentle voice to Laura, almost casually.

Stupefied, she watched him take a little bottle from his pocket, consider a moment, lay the obedient Andrew flat on his back on the ground, drop one drop of liquid in at each open staring eye, take a tape measure from his pocket, measure Andrew's position on the ground, pace a few steps away, mutter something, pace back; it went on and on. Laura's knees gave way and she sat on the grass. There were a lot of sheep still baa-ing . . .

Then with a patter of feet an immense flock began to pass down the lane accompanied by men and dogs and by the three or four cars which had willy-nilly become embedded in it. A very trim flock, cleaner and whiter than any Laura had seen before in this dale. They went on and on in a kind of subdued controlled rush and it was not until they had gone that she turned her head to look back at Andrew.

Mr Strange had gone. He was not to be seen anywhere. And Andrew suddenly yawned immensely and sat up and rubbed his eyes.

'Great God,' he said – Great God was one of the expressions current at his school that term – 'what on earth am I doing out here in my pyjamas? Have I been sleepwalking or something' I don't get it.'

Laura could have hugged him, he looked so cross and Andrewish. But she didn't.

'You do look rather daft sitting there; why don't you go in and change,' was all she said. And so that was what he did, disagreeable and snappish and certainly normal.

There is not much more to tell. Their mother, when she returned from her good gossip with Ann's mother at the farm which was where she had been for the past hour, was not so overwhelmingly delighted to see Andrew recovered as Laura expected because of course she hadn't realized how ill he had been in the first place. She merely said, 'Oh, I'm so glad you're about and feeling all right: now what would you like for tea?' and it was then that Laura began to realize for the first time how she would never, never be able to tell anybody what she had achieved because no one could possibly understand and believe her. Her whole terrible experience and adventure had been for herself alone. Andrew having forgotten, she could not share what she had done with another living soul.

For a moment the thought was so bitter she almost wished she could have been put in a sleep of forgetfulness herself and have done with the whole thing, but then she thought again that perhaps to have been one-quarter enchanted and to know it had yet been better than not having been enchanted at all. She had had such a view of the world as she would never forget, and though she hadn't exactly managed truly heroic behaviour all the time and would get no praise for the steadfastness she *had* shown she knew in herself what it was she had done, and that was enough.

That night she said to Andrew, just to test him, as he moved his things back from the spare bed in their parents' room: 'I wonder whether that funny old man is still about in the stables, I don't seem to have noticed him lately.'

'No, nor've I,' agreed Andrew, without much interest. He jumped on to his bed and gave one or two absent-minded bounces. 'I say, that hurt. Bother this silly ankle. I know what we'll do. Let's play cards. I found a pack in a drawer downstairs.'

'OK,' replied Laura happily. It was a long time since they'd had a good game of cards. 'What shall we play?'

By more skilful questioning spread over the next couple of days, Laura found to her great relief that Mr Strange had finally done his disenchantment job very well, for Andrew remembered all the normal, surface things which they had done in the past few days and thought he had done them normally: the long walk on the moors he felt a little shamefaced about as he thought he had a sudden urge to go and find fossils on the high rocks, which were said to be a good place for them, and he knew he had set off obstinately in unsuitable weather, and had been stupid and mistaken about the whole business. The only gap in his mind was the one caused by his awakening and finding himself outside in his pyjamas, and he accepted that he had gone sleepwalking readily enough as he knew he had not been very well. He had been apt to do odd, delirious things when he was a little boy and had a fever. And he accepted that he could remember so little of the walk and of being brought down from the moors by the schoolmaster because he had a kind of idea that he had been feeling rather odd all that day.

The only thing Mrs Hearst said at all about the disappearance of Mr Strange was a remark to the effect that she had better write to Mrs Anderson and tell her that her loft had been used by a tramp for a few nights.

'After all, she doesn't want the place turned into a doss-house for the down and out,' she said. 'Though that doesn't seem very likely up here. What are you and Andrew going to do today, Laura? Remember we're off back home tomorrow. Would you like me to give you the money for another pony trek if they can fit you in? You haven't been out on the ponies as much as I thought you would, in fact.'

'Yes, *please*,' returned Laura eagerly. She didn't mind how fat and woolly the pony would be; she would just enjoy being on it and being carefree.

Before she went off to the pony trekking farm to fix the ride she ran on an impulse up the stable steps and looked through the door. Yes, it was bare, empty, just as she had seen it with Ron and Cath. He might never have been there. In one corner something attracted her eye: a broken piece of china. It was gilt and white, only a fragment. It might have been the back of a cherub's head. It might not. Suddenly she shivered and dropped it.

'Come on, I'm coming to the pony place with you,' called Andrew from the field. 'I don't mind having another ride. It won't hurt my ankle now it's almost well.'

And so the holiday ended as it had begun; and agreeably,

with ponies. But that last night Laura dreamt a dream.

She was among sandbanks, ankle deep in soft sand. She could not see the sea, but she knew it to be near, beyond the next line of dunes. A little coarse grass grew in tussocks on the tops of the dunes, and behind her were a few scrubby bushes, bent and twisted by the wind. Behind that somewhere was a pale gleam from what she knew to be a desolate expanse of ice and thin snow and scrubland. There were no hills, it was all flattish country. There was no sign of life anywhere: no houses, no animals, no birds. The sky was high and pale and sunless. The only movement came from a little knot of midge-like flies which danced in a spiral above one of the tussocks of grass. The only sound was a very faint keening whispering sound: of the sea, and of wind over ice some miles away. On looking down she found she was walking slowly not through pure sand as she had imagined but through innumerable tiny bones and fragments of bone. She was crumbling them as she trod into yet smaller fragments. As she realized this in dismay a voice reverberated in her ears: 'This is a dying world.'

Loneliness pressed about her heavily, but she felt no panic, rather an empty calm, a feeling of inevitability: a kind of recognition: 'Of course I am very old. I have seen a great deal and now it is nearly over: nothing matters very much as far as this thing I call myself is concerned.'

Then, in a sudden shock, it struck her. 'But I'm *not* old. I'm a young girl,' and following upon the sense of personal identity, all the rush of a strong young personality taking over her body again, she began to wake, and as she woke, seeming to float up from fathoms deep, another voice tolled like a bell: 'The watchers are all gone now; the enchantment is over: the world is empty again.'

And Laura awoke as Laura, finding for some totally unexplainable reason that she wanted to cry; that she had lost something, she knew not what, a feeling only partially cured by breakfast.

'Well, you do look down in the dumps today,' said her

mother briskly, clearing the table. 'Have you done your packing? It's a great shame our holiday is over, but never mind. It's been beautiful up here, hasn't it? Though perhaps a little on the quiet side. Speaking for myself, I've had a lovely rest, but on the whole I think I prefer Cornwall. There is more going on there, somehow.'

But then she had not met with an enchanter.

## Nina Beachcroft
**Well Met by Witchlight** 60p

Sarah, Christopher and Lucy soon got used to having a witch for a friend. She was the nicest sort of witch, eccentric, but on the side of good causes. Her bewitching powers had been fading until the children encouraged her to take them up again . . .

## Leon Garfield
**Garfield's Apprentices Book 2** 60p

Three more stories in Leon Garfield's splendid series – recreating the colourful life of the London streets in the eighteenth century. 'The Cloak': the story of Amos and Jeremiah, sharp-witted apprentices in the pawnbroking trade. 'The Valentine': the story of little Miss Jessop, the undertaker's daughter. 'Labour in Vain': the story of Gully, the bucklemaker's apprentice.

## Mollie Hunter
**The Ghosts of Glencoe** 70p

Amidst the thick snows of February, under the shadow of the great mountains of Glencoe, the red-coated soldiers came in the dead of night . . . They had their orders – to turn on the homes of the Macdonalds and slaughter every man, woman and child. It was one of the most infamous and brutal massacres in history. For Robert Stewart, the young red-coat officer, it meant a fearsome choice – between carrying out his orders and abandoning his military ambitions in a desperate attempt to save the doomed clansmen . . .

## Sinéad de Valera
**More Irish Fairy Tales** 60p

Ten more strange and wonderful stories of magical spells and emerald trees, of witches and mighty kings . . . from the land of pixies and fairies and the strangest of sorceries.

Farley Mowat
**Lost in the Barrens** 75p

Jamie, the orphan who lives with his trapper Uncle Angus, and Awasin, the Cree Indian boy, are caught by the lure of exploring the great Arctic wastes. They join a Chipeweyan hunting party into the wild and come across a mysterious cache of relics from the distant past . . .

**The Curse of the Viking Grave** 75p

This thrilling adventure really began when Jamie and Awasin, the Cree Indian boy, found the strange cache of ancient relics described in *Lost in the Barrens*. With their friend, the Eskimo Peetuk, Jamie and Awasin set out into the wild north of Canada to rediscover their strange find. They come across the remains of the Vikings who reached North America centuries ago – the eerie contents of the Viking Grave . . .

compiled by E. Richard Churchill
**The Six-Million Dollar Cucumber** 50p

A bookful of zany riddles about birds, beasts and vegetables!

What can a canary do that an elephant can't?
Take a bath in a saucer!

When is it bad luck to have a black cat cross your path?
When you're a mouse!

And what is green, has one bionic eye and fights crime?
The Six-Million Dollar Cucumber!

Pages and pages of zany and hilarious riddles – for hours of fun.